For Dea and Phil,

Virginia Elaine Sievers

Sunshine on Water

The Unsettling Story of Callie Sue Hannamann

A Novel

Virginia Sievers

Sunshine on Water: the Unsettling Story of Callie Sue Hannamann
All Rights Reserved.
Copyright © 2021 Virginia Sievers
v3.0r1.1

This is a work of fiction. Names, characters, businesses, places, events, locales, and incidents are either the products of the author's imagination or used in a fictitious manner. Any resemblance to actual persons, living or dead, or actual events is purely coincidental.

The opinions expressed in this manuscript are solely the opinions of the author and do not represent the opinions or thoughts of the publisher. The author has represented and warranted full ownership and/or legal right to publish all the materials in this book.

This book may not be reproduced, transmitted, or stored in whole or in part by any means, including graphic, electronic, or mechanical without the express written consent of the publisher except in the case of brief quotations embodied in critical articles and reviews.

Outskirts Press, Inc.
http://www.outskirtspress.com

Paperback ISBN: 978-1-9772-3428-5

Cover Photo © 2021 Shutterstock
Cover design by Carl E. Sievers - All rights reserved - used with permission.

Bible verse from King James Version

Outskirts Press and the "OP" logo are trademarks belonging to Outskirts Press, Inc.

PRINTED IN THE UNITED STATES OF AMERICA

sunshine on water

welcome courier
of quiet serenity
harbinger of calm

engaging envoy
of hopeful times
prediction of promise

unwanted messenger
of forlorn despair
omen of disaster

Emma Betz here.

Longtime resident of Hamburg, town librarian, and writer of Callie Sue's story.

Yes, it's true. I'm the writer of Callie Sue's story.

I suppose this is a surprise to the community because I'm known as an established librarian rather than as a writer of stories. I have no yearning to put words on paper and have never had that yearning.

That is, I've had no yearning until now.

Working late at my checkout desk here in the Hamburg Library, rereading what you're about to read, I'm reflecting on how this venture came about. Considering my wanting writing qualifications it was brave, and surely naïve, for me to step into this unfamiliar territory.

Quite simply, I thought Callie Sue's story should be told. Because her story could relate to any one of us it would be meaningful to readers. It would also be timely, as its disturbing focus is front page news these days. There was another reason for writing. It's a reason of personal importance to me, as you will understand later. I wanted Callie Sue's true story to come out. Publication of the true story would put an end to the unfair and unkind gossip floating about.

Having established in my mind that the story should be told, I gave myself good reason to be the one to tell it. I'm the only outside-of-the-family person in our community who knows the true and full story. If it's to be shared with the world, I should be the one to share it.

I envisioned a plan. This wouldn't be a modest little tale about a local teenage girl with a problem. Even with my writing inexperience I could give my readers an offering with more depth than that of a simple tale. I'd look into the big picture of what happened and how it happened. I'd keep the focus on Callie Sue but spend time exploring feelings and attitudes of family members, and I'd delve into family relationships and histories as well. I'd definitely rummage into the workings of our beloved Midwest farm community where Callie Sue spent her formative years. This would be an all-embracing story, heartfelt and not easily forgotten.

The idea of writing Callie Sue's story hung around, pestering and making itself bothersome. It wouldn't go away. Finally, once again I told myself, "This story needs to be told," and with a burst of unexplainable ego I added, "and it needs to be told *my way*."

So last winter I tackled what was for me a daunting task. I sat down and wrote Callie Sue's story. I didn't stop writing until I'd said it all, and said it to my liking.

I have good feelings about this venture. Admittedly the actual writing gave me some setbacks, with unexpected snags and pitfalls along the way. But I endured, and in the end the account says what I want it to say.

I'm pleased you're reading Callie Sue's story and can tell you, positively, that she would be pleased as well. She would encourage you to read with a tolerant mind, and to ponder the story when you've finished. She'd want it to linger in your head, to become a part of your cache of references on the subject of evil.

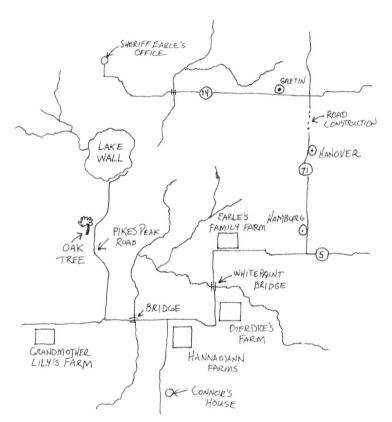

PROLOGUE

Until she was fourteen, Callie Sue Hannamann spent her growing up years on Hannamann Farms, her family's prosperous Midwest farming operation.

You'll read more about the farm operation but right now I'll mention that Hannamann Farms is a beautiful layout, built up through the years by proud past family generations and destined to be handed down to coming family generations. The operation is what we in the community call quality. The land is rich and productive and it's managed with sound business sense.

Sometimes we get a little envious of the operation and its proud ownership by the Hannamanns, and in our envy we look for something to take the family down a notch or two. But that doesn't mean we wanted this thing with Callie Sue to happen. Being envious doesn't mean being hateful. We respect the

Hannamanns and they respect us.

Besides, as is usually the case in small communities, we understand each other.

Mostly we understand each other, Callie Sue being an exception. Callie Sue was hard to understand. An enigma is what she was. One could say she was the square peg that didn't fit into the round hole. If there's one thing we like here in the community it's having all the pegs fit, so it was most bothersome to us that she didn't. Believe me, her not fitting caused some serious discussion and of course we all had our own ideas regarding why. We did agree on a couple of things. Callie Sue was a headstrong girl from day one, and she was used to having her own way.

Some folks would fault Callie Sue for what happened, but knowing what I know and what they don't I'll tell you right off I don't fault her. You'll soon see my mindset favors Callie Sue so you're welcome to come to your own conclusion as to what she was all about.

Some folks say she was defiant and disrespectful and hellbent on doing her own thing. Some folks say, "Just plain spoiled." But I say, on the positive side, that Callie Sue bounded through her growing up years with more energy than most. And she was pretty. "Too pretty," some say, so maybe being pretty didn't actually work in her favor. Callie Sue had another positive going for her. She was a born leader. She collected friends and admirers without trying, pulling them in like a strong magnet pulls in steel.

You'd look long and hard to find a child more loved and adored, and on her side Callie Sue harbored deep love for her family. Before this thing happened we didn't know about the untold love she had for her family. We thought the love went all one way.

To understand Callie Sue's story you should know something about Hamburg and our farming community, since the customs and traditions of a setting are compelling predictors of attitudes and behavior. It was certainly so in this case. I can tell you our Hamburg's a quiet Midwest town that's been here a long time, nicely situated on the banks of the Little Raccoon River. (The Little Raccoon's more like a big creek than a river, but whatever. We like calling it a river.) The town nestles into the surrounding farmland like a nest nestles into a tree, which is to say it's a secure and cozy place to be.

Hamburg draws us in, giving us our rightful place in life. It draws the farm folks in as well. The Hannamanns and their neighbors drive to Hamburg to bank and do business and they come here to church and to the library. The children come in on buses to school. The farmers support the town and the town supports the farmers, and since we like each other and get along fine I'd say we're together as one in our cozy nest.

Having history in Hamburg and being the librarian, I know most of the people here and I know a good share of the families on the farms. I've known the Hannamanns for years: Otto Hannamann before he died, and Lily, too. Walter and Eva Hannamann and their children, Callie Sue, Anna, and Little Otto. And I know Eva's cousin, Sheriff Earle Meier, because his mother's a Dorman, the same family name as my great aunt. This means Sheriff Earle and I are shirttail relatives. Lots of folks around here are shirttail relatives, related from way back. I also know Eva's sister, Dierdre Bonhoff, and I knew Elise Freidrich, their mother, although the Bonhoffs and Freidrichs don't count as Hannamanns.

In our part of the world we like things the way they are and we aren't in a hurry to change them. Habits are deep-seated and routine suits us fine. Life inches along in a predictable way. That is to say, the sun comes up and the sun sets and the seasons come and the seasons go, and occasionally there's something to get excited about but not very often.

When you get to know us you figure out we don't take to frivolous ways. Serious is what we are, as in keeping our noses to the grindstone and saving our money. Also serious as in watching out for each other.

There's that, too. Seems like word spreads like wildfire when something noteworthy or conspicuous happens, and we're right there to support or help. Sorry to say, though, that sometimes tongues wag the wrong way, the word gets twisted and 'before you can say Jack Robinson' it's way out of kilter. This is a thing we aren't proud of, this tendency to get things out of kilter. We don't like owning up to it, but it happens.

It's been ten years since the August day that surprised, ambushed really, the unsuspecting Hannamanns. It was late summer when life was ambling along at a nice steady pace. The day wasn't particularly memorable in itself but we remember it because it was the day there was trouble out at Hannamann Farms. It was a day we got excited.

Since there's all manner of speculation about what happened, with not one of the speculations grounded in truth and some of them with twists and turns where they shouldn't be, I want the real story to be told. Told the way it actually came down, not out of kilter, and told from a reliable source. That would be from me, Emma Betz. I'm plainspoken and honest and folks trust me. Sometimes folks don't appreciate that I hit the nail on the head and call a spade a spade, but they don't have trouble believing what I say. My record's unscarred when it comes to telling the truth. If Grandfather Betz were still living today he'd tell you fair and square, "By golly, with our Emma you can take truth to the bank."

So you can be sure I'd be telling Callie Sue's story like it came down, plain and simple without embellishments or little gems of embroidering to soften its hardness or make it more palatable.

Last winter when the snow was blowing and the cold outside was frightfully bitter and folks didn't get out much to come to the library, I had extra time. I put on my heavy purple sweater to keep warm and sat down at my checkout desk out near the drafty entrance hall and got started. I kept at it. Wrote every day. I concentrated on each person's story as I saw it, and before I knew it the stories pieced together into a full account that pretty much says it all.

This story begins in August of '97, right here in our nice quiet farm community. In the musical, *The Music Man,* we're told, "It happened right here, folks. It happened right here in River City." That's how it was with us. Callie Sue's story happened right here in our own little river (creek) town of Hamburg. It happened right here under our innocent and unsuspecting small-town noses.

Who would believe? Sometimes I can hardly believe it myself.

The Hannamanns

The Uncle

August, 1997

"Self-importance is the worst sin
 a person can get into."
Rajesh Nanoo
Indian Author and Poet

Without the fanfare and show typical of his driving behavior, Sheriff Earle Meier eased his cruiser out of the parking lot by the Hermann County Sheriff's Office, then turned east onto County Highway 14. Prompted to action by the frantic telephone call from Eva Hannamann that came in a few minutes ago he slipped out of his office, locked the door behind him and now is headed out to Hannamann Farms.

When the call came Earle wasn't sure what to make of it, and as he turned onto the highway he was still trying to figure it out. This situation could be serious. Then again, maybe not. He needs to think about it.

First off, how serious the situation is forces an immediate decision on how to make the trip. Given his destination to the premier farm operation of the county that also just happens to be owned by his relatives, this coupled with Eva's urgency, he can easily rationalize putting on his siren and lights and tearing across the county at breakneck speed. But he isn't sure about the urgency. He knows Eva well and is aware of how she can make a mountain out of a molehill.

If this is a real mountain he needs to get there in a hurry. If it's a molehill there's no need to rush, and it's probably not a good idea to advertise the trip either.

Earle has his own idea of what happened. If he's right, and he's pretty sure he is right, instead of making the big scene he likes with flashing lights and a screaming siren he can keep his foot light on the gas, drive slow, and use the extra driving time to good account planning what to say and how to say it when he gets to the farm. He knows one thing for sure. The 'how to say it' part needs to be planned with care. What's ahead might not turn out to be a dire emergency but it could well turn out to be a fragile situation.

He decided in favor of restraint, without the lights and siren. Better to not make a scene. Better to take his time and think this thing through, and if his hunch is right be prepared when he gets there.

Earle settled into unhurried driving. Anyhow not a bad thing to take his time on this late August day with crisp fall days waiting just around the corner. No wind, just pleasantly warm and balmy. "My kind of day," he thought with satisfaction. "My kind of country," he added proudly, anticipating the morning drive ahead through the farm country he knows so well.

His shiny white sheriff's cruiser, with *Earle*

Meier: Hermann County Sheriff painted on its doors, passed fields of ripening corn and soybeans as it eased down the highway. As his planning project sped along at full speed in the back of his head, up in the front of his head Earle couldn't help taking note of the crops, admiring them, and talking to himself about yields. "Maybe an overall average of a hundred and fifty bushels of corn to the acre this year, give or take a few bushels. The soybeans look fantastic, the best I can remember. The price of soybeans is soaring, so a high yield coupled with the rare selling price will be a nice payoff for the farmers."

A smile came then. His mother often said, "Earle will always have an interest in the crops. You can take the boy out of the farm but you can't take the farm out of the boy." She was right on. He didn't end up farming but he'll always love the farm, and he keeps up with what's happening out here in the country.

"If nothing catastrophic happens like a hailstorm or an early frost it'll be a bumper crop," Earle decided. He's glad for the farmers. "I'm glad for myself," he admitted, knowing that if the farmers are prosperous the community's prosperous, and if the community's prosperous people have fewer reasons to break the law.

Earle kept his foot light on the gas, staying just below the speed limit. At least folks won't get excited about speed when he passes the farmsteads. It's common knowledge the farm women keep track of highway traffic from behind curtains and the men look up from their outside work to see who's driving by. At the noon meal they talk about it. They ease into the subject with feigned innocence but if you know these farm folks, and Earle does know them, there's no question gossip is coming. It starts with a tentative drawl. "Saw Sheriff Earle drive by this morning," or "Wonder where Sheriff Earle was headed this morning." Then there's speculation about where he's headed, and after everyone at the table has a say and no one ever really figures it out, they stretch out the talk to explore his history. Like last year when he went tearing across the county with his siren and lights on in pursuit of a young kid who raced through an intersection's red light and wouldn't stop when the sheriff's car tailed him. That story's told time and time again at the noon meal and you can be sure it's told one more time when Earle's name comes up.

The attention pleases Earle even if he isn't at the farm table to bask in it. Just knowing he's the subject of conversations like this pleases him. When things are slow he lets the attention go to his head, but today his head's occupied so he keeps his vanity in check.

Eva Hannamann is Earle's second cousin. The call from Hannamann Farms this morning was her doing. The minute he stepped into his office the phone rang, cutting into the silence with shrill insistence. Hearing the ringing didn't please him and he was irritated to have to answer because he'd set aside today to do office paperwork and he likes doing it at his own pace, without interruption. But what do you do? A job's a job.

Eva got right to it when he answered. "Earle, we have trouble out here. Can you come?"

Earle sat up and listened, ready for the worst. "That's how it is when you're the sheriff," he told himself. "You have to be ready for any situation at any time." Behind the bravado he shows the world when he gets a call, Earle's heart races and adrenalin pours in, preparing his body for battle. It's *fight* or *flight*, and although he might want to he doesn't choose flight. Not this sheriff. This sheriff, even with his fancy blustering and posturing, works hard to keep up his official image.

"What's going on, Eva?"

"Oh, Earle, Callie Sue's gone. She didn't come home last night and we haven't heard from her and we're worried and we've tried to figure it out and we can't understand where she can be and we keep looking and …"

"Hold on, Eva," Earle said into the phone. "One thing at a time now." Eva has a habit of talking in long sentences without periods, inserting 'ands' where the periods should be. Especially when she's excited she leaves out the periods and for sure she's plenty excited right now. "Start at the beginning. You say Callie Sue didn't come home last night?"

"She said she wanted to walk over to Dierdre's to help her pick tomatoes and then they were going to freeze them and it was about three o'clock when she left here and she didn't come home." Earle sensed Eva was close to tears. A pause and then, "You know what? Dierdre says Callie Sue didn't show up and the two of them didn't have a plan to pick tomatoes or freeze them either and Dierdre says she hasn't talked to Callie Sue for two or three days. Oh, Earle, we just can't figure this out and…"

Eva was about to go on with another long sentence but Earle interrupted. "Eva, let me talk to Walter."

"He's not here. He's out driving around looking for Callie Sue and he was going to stop at neighbors and then drive into town and ask around."

Earle looked at the clock. He needs to check this out. Eva's family and she's family he likes a lot. Sometimes she gets upset when she shouldn't but she's one good person, good as gold, and if you don't believe it ask people in the community and they'll tell you the same thing. Earle considered his schedule.

His paperwork can wait so no reason not to drive out to the farm right now. He doesn't like office work anyhow. What he likes is dressing up in his uniform and cruising around in his fancy sheriff's car.

"Eva, I'm pretty busy here but I'd better come on out." He looked at the clock on the wall. "If I leave now I'll be there in an hour, maybe a little sooner. You keep looking. Call Callie Sue's friends. Maybe she stayed with one of them." He went on. "Try to think back on what she's been up to lately. Think about who she's palling around with or if you've noticed anything different or strange."

He could hear the relief in Eva's voice. "Earle, thank you so much and Earle we're so worried and you know how pretty Callie Sue is and you know she likes pretty things and we try so hard to keep things going right for her and…"

Earle interrupted again. "Eva, you hush now. I'll be there soon." He told her goodbye, glad the call was over. Eva's a love but she does go on.

So now, instead of working in his office like he planned Earle's on his way out to Hannamann Farms. Taking his time, turning over in his head this problem with Callie Sue. As he approaches the City Limits sign of the small town of Greten he slows down even more, drives through at a snail's pace, and is in the country again.

He knows what happened, or he's pretty sure he knows what happened. Not hard to figure out. Callie Sue ran away. A fourteen-year-old girl pretty as pretty can be. Likes the boys. Doesn't like the farm. Doesn't do as well as her little sister in school. Doesn't actually like school much. School starts in a couple of weeks so if she runs away now she doesn't have to go.

A sly look in her eyes. Crafty. Wily.

Not a bad kid, though. Aren't a lot of fourteen-year-old kids up and down and all over the place?

Earle dreaded telling Eva and Walter what he thought. "Oh, Lord. They won't like this," he told himself. The Hannamanns like routine and live by habit. They don't break or even bend their rules and they don't mess with the unspoken rules of the community either. Their Callie Sue's been breaking a lot of rules lately, so Earle hears. Not just breaking the rules but shattering the rules, and she's also doing her level best to thumb her nose at the community. So Earle hears.

Earle figures it to be about ninety percent sure Callie Sue ran away. Hermann County has an occasional runaway so he isn't a beginner in dealing with the situation. When it happens he puts out a state alert but he wouldn't even need to do that. The runaways come back on their own in a day or two or they show up at a friend's house, the parents embarrassed to have called him.

No reason to think this situation won't be the same.

Earle knows the Hannamanns well. He remembers when Callie Sue was born, Eva and Walter's first child, and he remembers her as a feisty little toddler. Now he thinks of her as a rebellious teenager. He's been at Eva and Walter's table many times, along with Callie Sue and Anna, the little sister, and Little Otto, the brother. Can't even count the holidays he's spent at Hannamann Farms when the entire clan was there. Fine virtuous people from way back. Now Eva out there working for every good cause in the community and Walter not having it any other way.

Coming up on the City Limits sign of the larger busier town of Hanover Earle braked for the new highway construction, raising his hand to the workers even if he doesn't know them. Can't hurt to let them see the sheriff driving by. The construction company brought along its own people but Earle figures it could have filled in with boys in the area who need summer jobs. There are too many outsiders around for the summer. So far no problems and he's hoping it stays that way but you can never be sure about outsiders.

He drove on and into Hamburg, looking down Main Street for Walter in his black pickup out looking for Callie Sue. Walter's wasting his time. It won't do any good to look. The girl will be far away by now since it was three o'clock yesterday when she disappeared, and she wouldn't leave without a plan.

When Earle headed out of Hamburg on County Road 5 it was into familiar territory. Not so far now to Hannamann Farms. He drove past his mother's farm, in the family for a century and now farmed by his older brother, Elmo. His great-grandmother knew Hannamann Farms when it was just one farm of a hundred and sixty acres, belonging to Old Waldo Hannamann. That was before it was passed down to Otto, the son, and later to Walter, the grandson, and Earle expects one day it will go to Little Otto, the great-grandson, along with the other farms added to the estate through the years. The Hannamanns are big farmers now, a far cry from when Old Waldo homesteaded as a young man with his first hundred and sixty acres.

Almost there, Earle passed the building site of Dierdre Friedrich's farm. Now there's a case. She's Eva's sister and he doesn't care for her. Seems like no one cares for Dierdre. Like Eva, Dierdre's Earle's second cousin, but Earle guesses he isn't obligated to care for a person just because the person happens to be a second cousin. A sly one, that woman. Nothing like Eva. It's a long story and right now Earle doesn't want to think about the long story and anyhow it won't do a nickel's worth of good to think about it. It's water under the bridge.

The approach to the Hannamann Farms building site is always awesome to Earle and today, even preoccupied with how he's going to talk to Eva and Walter, isn't an exception. Unlike most farmsteads with ordinary graveled driveways, the Hannamann driveway is burnished concrete edged with brick, not in any way ordinary. It's bordered on each side with the magnificent well-trimmed mature oak trees Old Waldo planted years ago as seedlings, and the perfectly manicured grass beneath them extends all the way down to the blacktop mile-square road. Beside the heavy iron lane gate, open now for his arrival, is a large **HANNAMANN FARMS** sign, eye-catching with its bold black letters. Can't miss that sign.

Neatness everywhere. No rusted or outdated machinery left sitting around and no buildings in disrepair. The outer buildings are painted a quiet tan, except for the original recently refurbished barn now on the *State Historical Registry*, meant to stand out and painted the red of past times.

At the end of the burnished concrete driveway, standing tall and dignified like a queen looking over her realm, the large white farmhouse looks over the Hannamann property. The grounds are like a park in front of the house and Eva keeps a well-tended vegetable garden behind it. Just as Walter's an exceptional farmer Eva's an exceptional gardener, priding herself not only on her spectacular vegetable garden but also on her beautiful well-laid-out perennial garden, and especially on the huge pots of flowers by the front porch steps. Every summer she plants the pots in the same way with red geraniums and blue salvia, and she likes banks of free-flowing white alyssum pouring lavishly over the sides.

"The farmstead's beautiful," Earle thought. "A sight to behold."

Heralding a strong statement to the community it says, "Please take note. We're the Hannamanns. we're hardworking prosperous farmers and proud of it." So true. The family's remarkably and admirably industrious, is more than comfortably wealthy, and has pride to spare. There's no question Hannamann Farms counts big in this farming community.

Earle drove around to the back of the house and there's Eva coming out the door to meet him. He knows she's been waiting for him, watching from her kitchen window for his cruiser to turn up the driveway from the blacktop road. Now here she is flying down the steps, her face clouded with worry.

He's ready. The slow drive allowing thinking time was a good idea, and now Earle Meier, Hermann

County Sheriff, has a plan for talking to Eva and Walter. He's immensely pleased with the plan and immensely pleased with himself for working it out.

He opened the door of his cruiser, stepped out, and put out his arms. Exhausted from a long sleepless night of worry, Eva Hannamann collapsed into them. Breaking into tears she sobbed, "Oh, Earle, she was here just yesterday and now she's gone…"

The Father

Three Years Later
August, 2000

"God hath yoked to guilt her
 pale tormentor, misery."
                    - William Cullen Bryant

Walter Hannamann...tall, soft-spoken and and deliberate, closed the machine shed behind him, sliding the heavy door on its runners and snapping the padlock down. It's late afternoon on Hannamann Farms and he's ready to call it a day. The predicted rain held off so he could finish spraying the forty-acre field behind the house, and now the air has a soft calm he likes. Some threatening clouds in the west but no breeze yet. Walter's always pleased with himself when he puts in a solid day's work and today's delay of the rain let him do it.

As he heard the click of the padlock he thought about how times have changed. How locking up is part of the routine he follows now at the end of his workday. When he and Eva moved from their first farm to the home place, the year Otto and Lily decided it was time for him to take over the operation and they traded building sites, they didn't lock doors. No one locked doors. To even think anyone would come in and steal was unheard of.

That was back then. Now Walter and his neighbors always lock their machine sheds *and* their houses, and they also lock their garages and cars. It's unheard of to not lock up. These days honesty isn't taken for granted.

Walter has his own reason for locking, a reason he's never mentioned to anyone. A strange, actually bizarre, incident happened three years ago, in the summer before Callie Sue ran away. Sometime over that summer, he guesses it was probably mid-July, his farm dog disappeared. Not a strange thing for a farm dog to disappear because dogs wander away sometimes, or join a pack, or just die out dogging around. Shep was old so most likely he wasn't dogging around, but no matter what the reason for the disappearance he was Walter's dog for a long time and losing him in any way was painful. When harvest time came in mid-October, when Walter was harvesting corn on the family's eighty-acre spread a mile down the road, he saw an obstacle in the row ahead. As the machine neared he could see it was a sprawled-out animal, and when he stopped he saw it was Shep, mangy and decayed. He'd been there awhile. Walter climbed down from the machine to pick him up. What he saw made him cringe. Shep's neck was slashed, a single perfect knife slash, clean as could be.

It looked like a murder, a dog murder, a purposeful act of violence to his beloved Shep. A low mean act of violence.

A temperate man given to cool reasoning who

would never harm an animal let alone kill one, Walter was shocked. Who would kill his dog? He didn't think he had an enemy. Was an intruder in the neighborhood? Maybe a road worker on the construction site at Hanover? Maybe someone wanting to steal machinery or livestock without the warning bark of a dog?

Walter buried Shep right there in the field and didn't tell Eva or anyone else. But the next day he drove into Hamburg and bought padlocks for the farm buildings and he had their hardware man, Hank Neilsen, come out from town to key the house doors. Eva didn't like it. She hated locking up and didn't see a reason for it, but Walter stayed on her case and in time she got into the habit of locking and carrying keys.

As he walked to the house from the machine shed Walter thought about the August day three years ago when they lost Callie Sue, and about how the heartbreak of the loss is always with him, ready to surface at any time. It's a deep dark despairing heartbreak that appears out of nowhere, like right now, tying his stomach in knots. He can hardly stand the pain.

Aside from August being the month of Callie Sue's impulsive revenge (*impulsive revenge* is what he's come to believe about her foolhardy decision to run away and damn her anyhow for bringing trouble on them), August brings a lull to the never-ending push of getting the crops in and on the way. At least that's good. He has time now to get the machinery ready for harvest, a small pleasure he's grateful for. He looks for small pleasures. "How will I go on if I don't look for small pleasures?" he wonders.

In years past Walter looked forward to August for another reason. The family went to the State Fair in August and after their day at the fair they headed up north to Black Hawk Lake, where they rented a cabin to spend a few relaxing days together before school began. Walter liked to fish and didn't often get the chance. On the lake days Little Otto trailed after him, begging to fish beside him. "Daddy, I want to fish, too," Little Otto said, looking up at him with trusting eyes. Walter patiently put a worm on Little Otto's hook and steadied his chubby little hands on the pole.

After Callie Sue ran away they didn't go to the State Fair. Callie Sue loved the fair. Walter remembers her excitement when he took her on the Ferris Wheel the first time. How she clung to his arm and wouldn't let him rock the seat, and then in later years she rocked the seat herself because she liked the thrill. Every year Callie Sue saved some allowance, planning ahead for a bag of mini donuts. How she loved to watch the machine plop the little donuts into the hot sizzling oil, and when she got her bag she savored each donut and made it last a long time. One year she started saving early, to treat Anna and Little Otto. Walter remembers watching all three of his children taking a break from the hot sun, sitting under the big oak tree by the fair parking lot eating their donuts and drinking Eva's lemonade and talking about their favorite rides on the Midway. Callie Sue had a protective bent when it came to her little sister and brother. She watched over Anna and Little Otto like a mother hen watches over her chicks.

Now they don't go to the State Fair and they don't rent a cabin at Black Hawk Lake either. Last year Walter told Eva they should rent a cabin but Eva was so pained when he brought it up he didn't mention it again. "Walter," she said, with tears in her eyes. "I've been thinking about it, too. I can't go. I'd like to go but I can't face being there without Callie Sue. Anna and Little Otto would like it and they would have such a good time and they deserve a holiday and I feel so guilty we didn't try harder and…"

Walter understood. Eva's right. They should have tried harder. They should have done something. Not their usual 'wait and see'. They shouldn't have let the problem simmer along while they hoped for a change. Hoped Callie Sue would miraculously wake up some morning and be happy. Hoped she'd get busy with her friends when school started and then things would be better. Hoped she'd outgrow whatever it was she was dealing with.

No question about it. They were big on hope.

There's another 'shouldn't'. They shouldn't have listened to Sheriff Earl tell them Callie Sue would come home on her own. Why the hell didn't they insist on trying to find Callie Sue, and trying to find her right away? They listened to Sheriff Earle, that's why. He's Eva's cousin, that's why. "Sheriff Earle's *family*," they said. At the time it was uncomfortable to question a family person's wisdom, or even make a suggestion.

Walter turned away from Eva so she wouldn't see his tears. She isn't the only one who feels guilty. He lives with guilt. Guilt in the morning when he wakes up and guilt at night before he goes to sleep and guilt in the hours between. A rotten way to live. A hell of a rotten way to live.

The day Callie Sue ran away Walter sprayed weeds, just like today. He came back to the machine shed about five o'clock to put the equipment away, happy with his work, tired, and ready for one of Eva's suppers. Probably scrambled eggs and ham and he knew she was baking her lemon cookies that afternoon. Walter remembers thinking, "Life doesn't get any better." All was so good. He loved farming and

Eva loved the farm and they had three healthy children who didn't give them trouble. Except Callie Sue lately with her headstrong stubborn rebellions, getting worse, but he still told himself she'd outgrow them.

He was foolish to believe she'd outgrow them. Now, looking back, he knows he was selfish as well as foolish. He didn't *want* to deal with his daughter's behavior. He didn't want to be bothered. The truth: "I wanted to be a farmer and take care of my land. I wanted to be left alone."

He remembers he was tired that afternoon and thought he'd call it a day. Just like today, he'd take a shower and put on his slippers. Maybe after supper he and Eva would sit on the porch and look out across the fields of corn and soybeans. For a farmer, August is the month to sit back and gloat (or complain) about crop yields and that year of '97 the crops were fantastic. He wanted Eva there beside him when he bragged about them. She probably got tired of listening to the stories he knew got bigger than they should, but Eva always listened faithfully and never failed to say, in one way or another, "Walter, you're one heck of a farmer."

Callie Sue wasn't at the table that night for the ham and eggs and lemon cookies and now Walter's ashamed to remember how pleasant it was without her at her place.

All that summer Callie Sue pushed, never letting up on her whining and complaining. Seemed like she waited for him to come to the supper table so she could unload to everyone there her disapproval of Eva and him. If it wasn't disapproval of them it was contempt for farm life or disgust with neighbors. Callie Sue made sure to sully the neighbors and she was ruthless about it. When she got started with one of her tirades, beginning with simple complaining before turning downright nasty, he got up and left the table. When he went outside his fists were clenched and his stomach hurt and he was furious at his impertinent kid. What the hell was the matter with her?

His heart went out to Eva. She had to take it more because she was with Callie Sue all day. One time when he came in for supper Eva met him at the door crying, giving her report to him in her own tirade of anger, in about ten sentences linked together with 'ands'. Eva didn't know what to do with Callie Sue. She was nearing the end of her rope and she was tired of it all. She'd had it with Callie Sue.

That night they talked it over before they went to sleep. "What's going on with Callie Sue? Is this a phase we didn't plan for? Are we doing something wrong?"

Eva wondered if they should talk to the school counselor but Walter wasn't one to ask for help or even admit they had a problem. Walter said they should send Callie Sue to her room when she got started and they should 'lay down the law'. He didn't say it, but he really thought he should give the little scamp a good swat. That's what he wanted to do. But they didn't hit their children, never had.

Besides, Callie Sue wasn't a little scamp anymore. She was a strikingly pretty fourteen-year-old girl.

In the end they didn't talk to the school counselor about Callie Sue's bad behavior and they didn't lay down the law either. In the end, they bit their tongues.

In the end, they endured.

"In the end we did nothing," Walter rued. "And look what happened."

The Little Sister

Four Years Later
August, 2001

"Youth comes but once in a lifetime."
    – *Henry Wadsworth Longfellow*

When the first edge of the sun appeared on the horizon bringing a touch of light into the open window, Anna stirred in her sleep and turned over. She nuzzled her head deeper into the pillow, grateful for summer mornings without the sudden ear-piercing ring of her alarm clock. Grateful for the quiet unhurried early dawn when the first noise is an occasional rustle of leaves in the oak trees.

Half-awake and savoring the silence, she waited for the sounds of the farm waking up. Mother's cocky old rooster crows at daybreak and Yeller runs at him and barks. The rooster crows again, taunting him, and Yeller barks again and growls his low guttural warning. It happens this way every morning. She'll hear Jake, the hired man, opening the door of the barn to start the morning chores. Her pony, Velvet, hearing him coming will neigh softly, anticipating breakfast. Soon Mother will be downstairs in the kitchen pouring water into the coffee maker and opening the door of the refrigerator for the bacon and eggs she cooks for the family every morning.

Anna snuggled down under her comforter, feeling secure in her bed and in her room. Fresh white ruffled curtains drape the windows and her bookcase is filled with books she loves and on the far wall is Grandmother Lily's antique desk, kept neat as a pin. The bedroom's all about her, Anna Hannamann, reflecting a sensible girl with her feet on the ground. People say she's twelve going on eighteen and they say it as a compliment. "Anna's a love," they say. "To be sensible and a love too, is a good thing."

As happens every day when she wakes up, summer or not, Anna's thoughts shift to Callie Sue. Thinking about Callie Sue the first thing every morning is a hangup she doesn't like. It's been going on a long time and she can't make it go away.

It isn't that she wants thoughts of Callie Sue to stay away from her head because she adored Callie Sue. Even though some memories have faded after an absence of four years, what she calls up now are glimpses of a big sister gently taking her hand and guiding her through the hard spots in life.

But every morning? Does she have to start every morning with Callie Sue?

Anna doesn't talk about losing her sister and no one fusses over her about it. They didn't say at the time and they don't say now, "We have to tend more to Anna's feelings because she's the little sister. She takes it hard." At the time Callie Sue ran away Mother and her dad and the relatives and the neighbors and all of Callie Sue's friends were engulfed in their own grief, going around crying and shaking their heads and hugging each other saying, "Oh, this can't be." But it did be. Callie Sue did run away and she didn't come back, and after some time passed most people tucked 'Callie Sue' into the back corners of their heads. Feeling sorry for the little sister didn't cross their minds. Even now, when they pull up the memory of that dreadful August day, they only deal with their own loss.

At first Anna thought her sister would come back. She imagined Callie Sue downstairs talking to Mother, saying she's sorry and how wrong it was to run away. Or one day there's Callie Sue walking up the driveway from the blacktop road, laughing and bragging about having a grand time in Chicago by herself. For a long time Anna imagined things like this.

Now the imagining's gone. Four years later the sensible little sister with her feet on the ground has given up on Callie Sue coming home.

Anna snuggled deeper under her comforter, glad for its warmth from the early morning chill. Connor comes to mind. Amazing how thinking of Connor makes her smile. Today she'll see him because it's his thirteenth birthday and their mothers are packing a picnic for their outing. She and Connor always spend their birthdays together, have spent them together every year since they were little kids.

Anna doesn't think it's strange her best friend's a boy and gets miffed if one of her girlfriends brings up the subject. Like, "Oh, he's your boyfriend, Anna. That's the reason you pal around with Connor." It isn't the reason at all because Connor isn't her boyfriend. He's just Connor and she likes him. They talk about anything and everything and he isn't silly like her girlfriends. Every day they ride on the bus to school together, Connor saving a place beside him when he gets on the bus because he lives six miles from Hamburg and Callie Sue lives four miles away.

Today Connor rode the two miles to Hannamann Farms on his bicycle. As he pedaled up the driveway in the morning shade of the oak trees he thought about the day ahead and knew it would be a good birthday. He counted blessings, clicking them off one by one. "It's my birthday. It was a great summer. I'm ready for school. Now Anna's waiting for me for our day at Lake Wall."

"Oh, Anna's your girlfriend," the guys tease.

Let them talk. He doesn't care. All he cares about right now is Anna's his best friend and he likes it that way.

There she is, waiting in front of the big white farmhouse with her bicycle ready, a brown bag of food in the basket. "Happy Birthday, Connor," she calls when he gets close enough to hear. Mrs. Hannamann comes out from the front door. He knows he'll be getting a hug.

A few hours into thirteen he's thinking, "Life won't get better than this."

Connor, a teen now, and Anna just three months behind, rode down the driveway to the blacktop road. Connor got off his bicycle to open and close the heavy iron gate and then they were off. They always follow the same familiar route for their rides and today's ride to Lake Wall takes them that way. Left to the bridge. Right at the next mile-square road. Down the little rise and up Pike's Peak Hill where they stop to rest and look over the countryside. Then Connor says, "Beat you to the oak tree," and they take off again, pedaling fast and riding like crazy.

After their rest at the oak tree, Lake Wall is still three miles away. Relaxing, riding along easy now, they talk.

"I'm missing Callie Sue," Anna said.

"I am, too," Connor answered.

"It's been four years. She's gone for good, I guess."

"Guess so."

Connor knows this is hard for Anna. They don't often talk about Callie Sue but when they do it's serious talk.

"I'm not sure she ran away," Anna said.

I'm not sure she ran away? What's this? Connor isn't sure he heard right. This is new and he isn't ready for new. Not today when he wants to enjoy every minute of his birthday. Anna's rattling him. In the last four years she's never once said, "I'm not sure she ran away."

He kept his voice even. "What do you mean?"

"I mean maybe somebody got her."

"You can't mean that."

"Sure I do. She wouldn't just up and leave. Well… maybe. But wouldn't she eventually come home? Or at least call?"

"How long have you been thinking this?" Connor asked. "Does anyone else think this?"

"A long time. Maybe a year. And I don't know what other people think."

As he often did, Connor took the lead to ride ahead. But the conversation troubled him. He dropped back to ask, "Have you told your mom and dad?"

"Are you kidding? Of course not. They wouldn't believe me. They'd tell me I'm wrong. They'd look at each other first and then look at me. With serious faces they'd put their arms around me and take a lot of time telling me they *understand* how much I miss Callie Sue. They'd tell me this is a natural reaction. That I *want* to think she wouldn't leave us."

They rode on, Connor thinking about Anna's bombshell announcement and Anna mulling over her parents' reaction if she tells them what she's thinking. They'd be kind, even if surprised. Aloud she said, "But before they finish setting me straight they'd make sure I'm okay. That, too."

"Well, are you okay?"

"I'm fine. I just feel bad. I always feel bad in August. You know that."

Connor does know, and he also knows when to be quiet and let well enough alone.

As he pondered what he'd just heard, Connor wondered if Callie Sue ran away on a day like this. He can't remember the day, exactly. That August day four years ago could have been sunny with a touch of fall in the air. Like today, the sky could have been a breathtaking blue, stretching as far as a person could see and dotted here and there with white fluffy clouds.

Now he'll have to say, "Callie Sue disappeared," rather than, "Callie Sue ran away." He guesses he can do that. He doesn't believe Anna's story for a minute but it isn't important what he believes. He cares about Anna and respects her. And he won't talk about it to others. Thirteen's a good age to be responsible for keeping a confidence.

Anna and Connor rode the rest of the way without talking, the companionship comfortable. When they came up on Lake Wall, tired, they walked their bicycles to the cleared shoreline where a few cars were parked in the lot, along with a smattering of bicycles.

People from Hamburg and the surrounding towns drive out to the picnic area but usually the tables aren't all taken. Anna and Connor headed for a vacant table on the hill overlooking the lake. They walked their bikes up the hill, ready to rest and open the bags of lunch their mothers packed, but wouldn't for the world divulge what was in them.

Anna opened her bag and found a plastic container of the fried chicken her mother made for supper last night. She'd already guessed there'd be chicken because Connor loves her mother's fried chicken and her mother loves it when Connor has seconds and thirds. Along with the chicken were sandwiches in buns filled with thick slices of ham, and a package of carrot sticks. Her mother put in a small plastic tablecloth and paper napkins. Connor's mother sent two large carefully-wrapped cupcakes, along with a box of candles and a matchbook. And a bag of homemade chocolate chip cookies and a small cooler with four cans of orange soda.

They laid out the picnic quietly, somehow knowing the day was memorable. Connor crossing the line between adolescence and the teen years, ready to be on the other side. Anna there soon and, like Connor, ready to be on the other side.

"Ready to be on the other side and move along," she thought. Then she added in her head, "Ready to move along from what's going on at home. It must have been going on a long time and I didn't see it."

It's Callie Sue again. Of course it is. It's always Callie Sue, one way or another.

Anna's discovered her parents carry out a silent vigil. Every day they wait for a telephone call and look in the mail for a letter. Even check the driveway, looking up from their work to glance at it, hoping she'll come walking toward the house. They don't talk about Callie Sue. They never say her name but Anna can see the vigil takes up big spaces in their heads. While clinging to hope (unwarranted hope because not once in the last four years have they heard from her sister or even gotten a clue as to where she might be) they smile and laugh and keep up a constant happy countenance for the world to see.

We're the happy Hannamanns. Happy, happy, happy. Look at us. We're doing fine.

Anna and Connor ate slowly, savoring the food and savoring the day. A gift to be treasured, this last time together before school begins. After taking their time with the chicken and sandwiches they lit the candles on the cupcakes and made wishes. They ate them slowly while sipping on the orange soda, then sat in the shade of the ancient linden tree by their table, backs leaning against it, in no rush to start back.

They talked about school. Connor told Anna his plans for the year and Anna told Connor her plan to work even harder for the grades she needs for college. Anna talked again about Callie Sue. She told Connor about her parents' behavior and her disappointment in what they're doing.

Late in the afternoon after they'd exhausted conversation, after strolling down to the shores of Lake Wall to watch the soft glow of the sun on the water, after coming back to their tree to finish off the chocolate chip cookies and the last of the orange soda, Anna and Connor reluctantly packed up and started home. They rode past the fields of corn and soybeans in silence, listening to the quiet ripple of breezes wafting through the leaves on the stalks of corn, and admiring the long straight rows of ripening soybeans.

After a long rest at the oak tree, loathe to end their time together and stretching out the day for as long as they could, it was on home to Hannamann

Farms.

When Anna and Connor rode up the driveway in the cool late afternoon shade of the oak trees, Eva and Walter waited on the porch smiling and waving. Anna watched them, feeling sorry but with anger knocking on the door. "They're trying so hard," she thought, as she smiled and waved back.

Anna isn't reacting to her parents' behavior the way *Sensible Anna Who's a Love* would react. *Almost Thirteen Anna* feels downright deceived. Who would believe her parents are still giving their loyalty, over the top intense loyalty, to Callie Sue who isn't even here and only God knows where she is. When she and Little Otto are here. Right here, every day. Giving life their all.

"A tad of resentment on my part," she admits, "and more than a tad of jealousy. But all the same…"

Almost Thirteen Anna knows the waiting game isn't going away. Hannamanns don't change. No way will they give up their well-grounded and well-practiced fixation. Probably when she graduates from high school her parents will still be waiting for Callie Sue. Probably when she gets married and has children they'll still be waiting for Callie Sue.

Anna went with Connor when he walked his bicycle back down the driveway to go home, and this time she opened the iron gate for him. "I hope you don't get a big head now that you're thirteen," she teased.

Connor looked at her curiously. *Is Anna teasing? Anna doesn't tease. Well, now.* He stopped walking, looked her in the eye, and teased back. "You're just jealous…Anna Marie Hannamann."

Anna tossed back her head, smiled slyly, and retorted in like manner. "Never jealous of you…Connor Anthony Kruse."

Surprised, but pleased with the fun, Connor fired back in his best even voice, this time embellishing his retort with a crooked little sideways smile. "You should be…Anna Marie Hannamann." And then, on an impulse coming out of nowhere (later he couldn't believe it himself) Connor leaned toward Anna and kissed her smack on the lips.

Whoa there!

Embarrassed, before Anna could see the blush he felt spreading over his face, he quickly turned away, jumped on his bicycle and raced down the blacktop road, keeping his eyes ahead of him. Connor Anthony Kruse couldn't have pedaled faster if the devil himself was after him.

Anna was stunned. "Would you believe?" she said

to herself. "He kissed me, and now he's leaving without saying goodbye." She wasn't about to let it go. She called to him, still teasing. "Bye, Connor. See you soooon…"

Connor pedaled faster.

Feeling lighthearted and incredibly happy, Anna closed the gate. Taking her time, she pulled it across the driveway and snapped the latch, thinking that closing the gate brought closure to the summer as well as to the day.

Musing then, thinking about the end of summer and buoyed up by Connor's kiss, she thought. "Maybe it's time to close the gate on *Sensible Anna Who's a Love,* too. Maybe it's time for *Almost Thirteen Anna Who's Moving Forward.*"

As she walked up the driveway thinking about new possibilities, considering a new chapter in her life, it occurred to her it would be a nifty time to move forward without Callie Sue. She thought about her morning hangup and about how nice it would be to be rid of it.

She liked the thought of moving forward without Callie Sue. "It's a good thought," she decided. "It's the best good thought I've had all summer."

The Grandmother

Five Years Later
August, 2002

For all sad words of tongue and pen,
the saddest are these, "It might have been."
— *John Greenleaf Whittier*

Quiet Haven Retirement Home, where Lily lives now, occupies several acres on the outskirts of Hamburg. A nicely manicured lawn dotted with huge well-trimmed trees, there for ages and salvaged during construction, complements the sprawling one-story building. A pretty rose garden borders one side of the winding sidewalk leading to the front door, and etched into the stonework by the door, in fancy print, are apt words: ***"Grow Old With Me. The Best Is Yet to Be."***

Hamburg's proud of Quiet Haven. People drive past when they have visitors, slowing down to point out what they especially like, usually dwelling on its quiet dignity. After crowing about how their town cares for its elderly (by golly, that's the way it should be...any town worth its salt watches over its old folks) the drivers invariably add, "I'll probably end up here myself one of these days."

Lily Hannamann, Callie Sue's paternal grandmother, did end up at Quiet Haven, a permanent resident now for four years. Lily has the best of the offerings with a spacious living room, kitchen, bedroom, bath with a walk-in tub, and even a small sun porch leading out to the patio where she keeps her pots of flowers. Eva sees to it the pots are planted every spring, stopping by to drive Lily to Fritzmeier's Nursery to choose plants. She comes in from the farm the next day or so with potting soil and a trowel and together she and Lily decide what plants to put in what pot. Lily would rather be back on the farm tending flowers in her garden and helping Otto with his vegetable garden, but the pots are the next best thing.

Otto isn't here anymore. Otto Hannamann, Lily's beloved husband for fifty years, died six years ago.

It happened just after Thanksgiving. As always, they had Thanksgiving dinner with Eva and Walter at the home place and pretty much everyone in the immediate and extended family was there, including Callie Sue who was thirteen that year. It was a cold dismal November day with a brutal biting wind and not a trace of sunshine. On the drive over from their farmstead she and Otto commented on the stark bare look of the trees without the color of fall leaves.

Lily remembers Otto saying, "It might be a long hard winter since it's trying to start early." He was right on both counts. Winter did start early and it was hard, but not hard just because of the weather. It was the winter he didn't survive, and that winter Callie Sue was angry and caused trouble whenever she could.

Thanksgiving dinner was a big perfectly browned turkey with all the trimmings, a repeat of the year before and of many years before that. As always, Lily brought vegetables from Otto's garden, already stored for winter or canned on shelves or frozen in the freezer. That year she brought glazed carrots, corn pudding, and sweet potatoes baked with the crisp topping everyone liked.

The children sat at the extended table in the kitchen, glad to be together. There was teasing and laughing and once again the quest to outdo each other expressing repugnance for the Brussels sprouts Great Aunt Dorothy contributed every year. They looked forward to their banter. Planned ahead for it. Little George, Otto's brother's grandson, started things along. He sat up tall and announced, "These Brussels sprouts taste like spoiled sauerkraut!"

Then the clown of the group, Arvid Burmeister, wrinkled up his nose and whined in a squeaky voice, "Yuck, yuck, yuck," each yuck louder until the last one, when he stood up and shouted at the top of his lungs, "**Yuck!**" His cohorts, his partners in crime, laughed with approval even though they glanced uneasily at the door to the dining room, wondering if Great Aunt Dorothy heard.

In the dining room Otto blessed the food, giving his usual long and well-thought-out annual benediction thanking God not only for the food but for all blessings bestowed. The adults took their time eating and talking, most of the talk about crops and weather but with some gossip mixed in. Later in the evening after games and naps the women laid out a spread of turkey sandwiches and leftovers, including any pumpkin pie not finished off at dinner.

It was a happy time, that Thanksgiving dinner together.

It was the last happy Thanksgiving dinner the family had together.

Three days later Otto died in his sleep. A pillar of strength for his family, the best possible neighbor and a strong leader in the community, Otto Hannamann surprised them all. The family and the neighborhood and the town of Hamburg were shocked. "Not Otto Hannamann," they said. "That can't be."

People didn't know what to say. Some of them, feeling a need to respond and trying to be kind by offering Lily a word of benefice said, "A good way to go. That's the way I want to go. When I die I want to go in my sleep."

When they said this Lily was indignant. She didn't get to say goodbye to Otto and she was upset about it. Still is. "I hope you get your wish," she thought when people talked like that. "The sooner the better," she added in her head, bitterly unforgiving of what she took to be insensitive comments. It was bad enough by itself to lose Otto. Not getting to say goodbye made the loss even more heartbreaking. Almost unbearable.

So the winter was long and hard. In addition to being bitterly cold that year, Otto died and Callie Sue kept up her shenanigans.

It was the next August that Callie Sue ran away.

For a few months after Otto died Lily lived by herself in the big house on her farm, a few miles down the blacktop road from the home place. Lonely without Otto and missing him more than anyone knew she carried on alone, grieved alone, and filled the empty hours in the best ways she could.

Lily thought she was doing well enough, but every time Walter stopped by he kept at her to move to the new retirement home. "You'll have the company of other people," he said. He said it again and again, never letting up, and finally he won out. On one of her sad days in early spring when Walter was putting on pressure, Lily relented and told him to go ahead and make the arrangements.

Surprisingly, she isn't sorry. Quiet Haven's nice and Walter was right. She really isn't as lonely. She manages her own schedule, closing her door to company when she feels like being alone and leaving it open when she doesn't. She does, of course, have the biggest and nicest suite for her independence because the Hannamanns practically bankrolled the place. Not too shabby being queen of the hill. In this case, Grande Dame of Quiet Haven.

A few of the residents don't let her forget about Callie Sue running away, though. Like her hens cackling on the farm, they cackle. Can't resist 'picking a little'. It might be a sly comment at the dinner table. "So Callie Sue didn't ever contact home?" Sylvia Burmeister asks with pretended innocence.

Or, "We feel so bad about Callie Sue," the meddling Keplers just happen to mention as they walk down the hall with her. The comments are one-up reminders to Lily, informing her that even with the Hannamann name and the Hannamann money she isn't so special after all.

Lily supposes the busybodies will always be ready to bring up Callie Sue. She wants to say, "Mind your own business, you conniving old gossips," or "Why is it so important to bring up my granddaughter? Why don't you go sit on a chair and behave yourself?" That's what she said to Callie Sue when she was out of line.

Walter kept farming the land along with the other Hannamann land and this was fine with Lily. But he rented the house right away when she moved to Quiet Haven and this didn't suit her so much, this knowing someone else was cooking in her kitchen and sleeping in her bedroom. He rented it to a middle-aged man and his wife, with no children, and it seemed to work out. The man was friendly with the farmers and helped out when help was needed. When they first moved in Walter drove her out to meet the couple. The woman was cordial enough and made coffee (in Lily's cherished old coffee brewer) but being there was uncomfortable, and Lily told Walter she didn't want to go back. Anyhow, the couple didn't stay long. She was glad when they went back to Texas to the man's old job.

When Walter figured out she didn't like outsiders in the house he decided not to rent it again, although he fussed about letting a nice house stand empty. Regularly he drove over from the home place to check it.

Lily sat on her couch and thought about Callie Sue. Usually she tucked 'Callie Sue' far back in her head because thinking about what happened was still painful. There was anger too. She was still angry at Callie Sue for running away, just as she was still angry at Otto for dying and especially for dying without saying goodbye.

"I need to let it go," she thought. "It's been six years since Otto died and five years since Callie Sue ran away. But she knows from suffering through other years that August and Thanksgiving aren't easy times.

Today: the first day of August.

She closed her door. Tired and sad she sat on the couch, put her head back on a pillow and gave in to the anger and pain, and to the deep-seated sorrow she silently harbors.

Lily had a hand in Callie Sue's growing up years. She and Otto kept a home where the grandchildren were welcome, so Callie Sue and Anna and Little Otto were often with them. They were in the kitchen helping her bake cookies or staying overnight in the upstairs bedrooms or playing 'Go Fetch' out on the front lawn with Otto's old farm dog.

Eva and Walter were good parents, setting limits and expectations for their children. But somehow they didn't see there was going to be serious trouble with Callie Sue, who didn't have Anna's even Hannamann temperament or Little Otto's innate Hannamann sweetness. Lily guesses Callie Sue got her genes from

Eva's side of the family. It was obvious from early on she didn't fit with the predictable Hannamann ways. The child couldn't be reined in. Even as a little girl she was a horse on a tear, with wild pent-up energy. She bucked the Hannamann ways right off her back whenever she could get away with it, throwing her head back and looking wild-eyed at the world. And Lily could almost see the wheels turning when Callie Sue was contemplating doing her own thing, calculating in her head if the consequence would be worth it. She was a smart one, that Callie Sue.

Lily made it a goal not to give Walter and Eva advice but now she wished she'd spoken up. She could've said, "You know, maybe Callie Sue needs a few more choices," or "Not everyone fits a mold." She could have suggested (did think about it), "Callie Sue has good ideas. Maybe you should let her try them out."

And did Lily herself ever sit down with Callie Sue and tell her to be patient? That life would be better when she was older and had more freedom. Did Lily ever put her arms around Callie Sue and say, "There, there now, honey, let's talk this over, just the two of us?" She did not. She purposely looked the other way and watched Callie Sue festering and Eva and Walter not budging an inch. It was an impasse of stubborn wills.

Part of the problem, too, was that damned Dierdre, Eva's sister, who's certifiably off the wall. Everyone knows it. Eva and Walter should have known better than to let the hussy get her claws into their girl. Dierdre took more than an auntie's casual interest in Callie Sue, overdoing it to the point of taking Callie Sue under her wing. She had her stay overnight with her and they went shopping for far-out clothes at Gutenburg, sixty miles away. High heels for a thirteen-year-old? Inappropriate low-cut dresses? The sexiest low-slung tight jeans they could find? Really. They tried out new makeup with Callie Sue sitting in front of Dierdre's dressing table mirror, Diedre encouraging her to put on makeup that made her look like a street walker. Callie Sue tried on Dierdre's clothes and they looked better on her than they looked on Dierdre.

Callie Sue loved every minute of it. Ate it up.

After her time with Dierdre she went back home to Eva, who everyone knows is the world's dowdiest mother (Lily could never figure out why Walter didn't seem to care) and the two of them would have it out. Callie Sue told her mother she looked old and fat and frumpy and Eva told Callie Sue she should act her age and she was far too vain for a thirteen-year-old and shame on her, and then Walter got into the act and sent Callie Sue to her room crying for being disrespectful to her mother. In the year before Callie Sue ran away there were hateful confrontations every day and Lily supposes Eva didn't tell her about the worst ones.

No, Dierdre didn't help the situation. But neither did she, Lily, help. Or Walter and Eva either. There was enough blame to go around.

Lily sat for a long time on her couch, remembering. She remembered holding her first grandchild, the birthday parties through the years, the first day of school every fall when she waited with Eva for the school bus at the end of the driveway and Callie Sue came bounding off the bus all smiles. Callie Sue was a happy child for a long time.

Things could have been different.

Lily put her head back on the pillow. Unlike Eva and Walter who keep hope alive that Calle Sue will come back, Lily doesn't have their hope. Knowing her granddaughter's stubborn independence, she doesn't expect to see her for a long time. Maybe never.

They lost Callie Sue on the day she ran away but the truth is they lost her before that day. They lost her in all the years before, in day-to-day living on Hannamann Farms.

She's gone, and as it was with Otto, Lily didn't get to say goodbye.

The Aunt

Four Years Later
2001

'So live so that you can look any man in the eye
and tell him to go to hell."
— *Anonymous*

So...here I am. Callie Sue's Aunt Dierdre. *The* Aunt Dierdre. Picking up speeding tickets in my little red Mazda convertible. Wearing my heels and flaunting the ruffled short skirts I love, because they flip out when I walk.

Here I am. Callie Sue's Aunt Dierdre, who doesn't fit in. Callie Sue's Aunt Dierdre, the Resident Mutant.

I deviate.

The Hannamanns say I'm wild. I'm not wild as in promiscuous, although I've had more than one boyfriend, or as in smoking pot, which I don't. I'm wild because I differ from how they think people should be. I deviate from The Hannamann Way of Thinking which is inside the box, The Hannamann Way of Doing which is don't rock the boat, and The Hannamann Way of Living which is every day the same.

Thank God I'm not a Hannamann.

The Hannamanns don't trust me. They don't come right out and say they don't trust me but it's there. I'm sorry to say this, but since this thing happened with Callie Sue maybe they're right. Maybe

I'm not to be trusted.

I don't drive the right kind of car, the right kind of car being stuffy and nothing flashy, please. They don't mention my red convertible or compliment me on how beautiful or how classy it is. Instead they say, "You drive too fast, Dierdre. You're going to have an accident." Instead of making me feel good with a smile and a nice friendly comment like, "Pretty neat car you have there, Dierdre," the Hannamanns dodge a compliment by telling me I drive too fast. So sometimes I drive my convertible really, really fast past Eva and Walter's farm. I rev the engine at the corner of the mile-square road before their driveway. Then I step on the gas and roar past.

I don't dress appropriately for my age. Of course I don't dress appropriately for my age. To them, appropriately for my age means black pants paired with a polyester top and sensible shoes, preferably black. Appropriately for my age doesn't mean cute summer dresses and classy sandals. I happen to like cute summer dresses and classy sandals, and if the sandals are high-heeled that's all the better. I wonder how old they think I am? If I were thirty-eight going on seventy-eight I'd dress for what they consider appropriate for my age, but I'm thirty-eight going on twenty-eight so I dress for twenty-eight. On the other hand, I have a personal goal to still look sharp at seventy-eight. If they knew my goal the Hannamanns would say, "She won't make seventy-eight the way she drives."

I don't talk right. I don't mean talk properly with correct grammar. I mean talk *right,* as in what is supposed to be talked about. There are rules. I don't sit on the porch and recollect how much rain we've had this month, or mention, "It looks like rain tonight," or bring up, "They had a big rain over in Hardy County last week and we could sure use a nice two-incher and it'd be nice if it came with no wind or hail."

Walter says, "The crops are the best we've had for several years."

And Eva adds, "The price of corn's holding up." The next enlightening statement is (trust me, I know), "It'll be a good year if we don't get hail or an early frost."

This is the right way to talk. Same topics of weather and crops. Over and over again. Every day.

Could we just do something radical once like not talk about the weather and the crops?

Darling Callie Sue didn't fit in either. Eva and Walter and the whole damned family knew it but they evaded the subject. They made a decision to ignore her unique talents. Now that I think about it, maybe it wasn't a decision. Maybe they didn't even notice her talents. How could these stagnated people who weren't blessed with creative genes recognize that Callie Sue had incredible taste in clothes? How could they recognize that Callie Sue having oodles of friends without even working at it was a natural talent? If they did have inklings they ignored them, relentlessly molding their darling daughter, who danced to a different tune, into one of them. They wanted her to talk about the weather and the crops and wear ugly clothes, and someday drive a dull car.

In so many ways Callie Sue was screaming to be heard. She talked back or she sulked and for a while she even tried not eating. During the year before she left Callie Sue walked over to my farm whenever she could. She'd sit at my kitchen table fretting over the family restraints and sometimes she'd cry and sob about a run-in with her mother, and how she didn't think she could take it anymore. And then she'd make me promise not to talk to Eva and Walter. "Aunt Dierdre, please don't tell Mother and my dad," she'd plead as tears streamed down her face.

More than once I picked up the telephone to call Eva. I'd say, "Eva, I'm coming over right now because we need to talk. You need to listen to Callie Sue." I'd talk to Eva in plain language she couldn't possibly misunderstand. "You need to see your girl as the person she is," I'd say. Then I'd decide not to call because I promised Callie Sue.

What I really wanted to tell Eva, to scream at Eva, was, "Stop trying to make Callie Sue into a Hannamann." But I couldn't come out with that. It'd be hurtful. Whatever else they say about me, they can't say I go around hurting people on purpose. Because I don't.

So I didn't talk to Eva about Callie Sue. I kept my promise and kept my mouth shut and look what happened. Callie Sue's gone. Gone, gone, gone.

Damn it all to hell.

No one asked me if I knew where she ran. It didn't occur to the Hannamanns that I, Aunt Dierdre, Resident Mutant, might have some information. Even Earle Meier, egotistical pompous Elected Sheriff of Hermann County, didn't come over to my farm to talk to me about Callie Sue. Earle Meier gets something in his head and starts believing it for gospel truth. This time he decided right away my darling niece ran away and that was that so why bother to talk to me…or to anyone else for that matter. Swaggering around drunk with self-importance in his sheriff's uniform with imaginary honor badges plastered across the front, crowing like a know-it-all, he announced with self-satisfied authority, "Don't worry, folks. She'll be back soon."

And the Hannamanns bought it.

He was right about Callie Sue running away but

if he was so sure why wouldn't he try harder to figure out where she ran? And why wouldn't he talk to me?

Like, "Oh, don't be silly. Aunt Dierdre wouldn't be any help."

I waited, and one day went into another and it wasn't long before a week went by and still no one asked me what I knew. So I decided to keep quiet. I was steaming about being left out and it felt good to know something the Hannamanns didn't know. Like, in your face, Eva and Walter. You know?

Anyhow Callie Sue would call or write soon, whenever she and Buck found work and a place to live.

Well, the joke's on me. The joke, or backfire, or whatever you want to call it, is on me. When she made good on her plan to leave Callie Sue didn't call or write to me like she said she would. In the first weeks I told myself not to worry. It would take a while to get things settled. I waited for the mail every day. Then, with no word for a long time I had to admit the girl didn't intend to keep in contact. It was part of her plan not to write to me.

Callie Sue was sneaking out and running around on the sly with a twenty-three-year-old man working construction on the new highway. He wanted her to go away with him. I didn't take her seriously.

"Aunt Dierdre, I'll write to you," she said.

I said, "Sure you will, honey," humoring her. This running away thing is what kids threaten to do when things don't go their way.

How was I to know Callie Sue was that serious about this man, Buck? How was I to know the girl had a real plan with this man, Buck? For God's sake, how was I to know she'd even carry out a real plan with this Buck…if indeed she had a real plan?

"Damn you, Callie Sue."

"Damn you, *Buck Whoever You Are.*"

"Damn you both, Callie Sue Hannamann and *Buck Whoever You Are.*"

"Damn you both all to hell."

The Mother

Five Years Later
2002

"If you suppress grief too much it can well redouble."
— *Moliere*

Eva wakes up early every day, relieved the painful night is over.

It's comforting to hear the familiar early morning stirrings on the farm. She listens for the soft rustle of breezes in Old Waldo's oak trees and she likes hearing the first loud crow from her arrogant showoff rooster. Then she waits for Albert Johnson to rumble by on the blacktop road in his old black truck, on his way to work at the County Maintenance Shop. People say he hasn't missed a day of work in thirty years and she guesses it must be so.

Waking up early is a relief but it isn't a blessing. Waking up early means a long day stretches ahead and it takes some doing to fill those hours. Days are as hard to endure as nights and sometimes they're harder.

But at least waking up is an escape from the never-ending tossing and turning and the hated dreams. The rolling over to put her arm around Walter, pushing her body tight against his back as her head flails wildly from one memory to another. The getting up in the night, her body clammy and wrung out with panic.

How to solve the problem? She's tried. Lord knows she's tried. Maybe nothing will solve the problem.

Good morning Mrs. Hannamann good to see you and tell me about your week is there anything you want to talk about today…and Eva talks and the weeks go by and the desperate sorrow stays and she doesn't feel any better and after a year she stops seeing Dr. Griffith… her idea to stop no point in continuing the hour's drive to Ulm.

On this day Eva has a plan.

These last years she's smarter about devising a plan for each day. Something to look forward to. Something to get her through. Anything as long as it works. A drive into Hamburg to visit Grandmother Lily at Quiet Haven. Pick strawberries and make freezer jam to take to Arvid Munson, their neighbor three miles north who lost his wife to cancer after fifty years together. A drive into Hamburg, this time to Holmgren's Bakery. Buy something. Stop at White Paint Bridge on the way home. Lean over the railing to watch the shallow creek water below trickling over the stones. Wonder how it would be to trickle along with the water, to keep going, to never come back. Come home and have coffee and the something from the bakery with Walter at the kitchen table.

Having a plan usually works.

Not always, in which case there are small tried-and-true backups. Take a walk down the driveway to the blacktop road and back, one foot in front of the other. Turn around and do it again. Make the round three times. Don't break the pattern.

On this day the plan is to drive to Dierdre's farm and sit with her over a cup of coffee. Walter doesn't like for her to visit Dierdre and Eva knows Lily wouldn't approve either, if she knew. Probably Walter has told Lily, though. Probably Walter and his mother have talked it over.

"Eva, you're going to feel bad if you go to Dierdre's," Walter will say. Or he'll ask, "Eva, why do you want to go there?" The 'go there' meaning hashing over memories of Callie Sue. Not go there to Dierdre's farm. Or maybe Walter means both.

If Lily knew Eva's going to Dierdre's today she'd press her lips into a thin line and not say anything. Maybe she'd say, "Oh." Just, "Oh." That's all. Her face disapproving even if she's careful with words.

Twenty years Eva's been married to Walter Hannamann but still an outsider in the family and nothing to do about it. They're a tight group, the Hannamanns. They think she isn't very smart and maybe they're right. Probably they have other describers like *naïve* or *sweet* (as in sweet because she doesn't like competition, not a good thing to not like) and *frumpy*.

For sure, *frumpy*.

Eva doesn't rock the boat. She's never rocked the boat. That is, not until lately she's never rocked the boat. She has to admit going to see Dierdre, making an effort with Dierdre, is rocking the boat. She keeps going, is stubborn about going, in spite of Walter's persistent opposition. She feels better when she sits with Dierdre at her kitchen table drinking coffee and eating the prune and apple kolaches they both like.

Walter could be more understanding. He already knows she's having trouble going to bed at night and getting up in the morning and he knows she's having trouble getting through the days. Walter could at least make an effort to understand her list of plans and she's aggravated he doesn't.

But he wouldn't be pleased to know that driving down the road to Dierdre's for coffee is the best plan she has.

Eva and Dierdre, the Freidrich sisters growing up together in a small modest house in Hamburg, inseparable back then. Their dad not amounting to much, seldom with a steady job. On the jobless days making his way to Charlie Schmidt's Main Street Café to gossip and hash out the morning news with his coffee pals. Their mother cleaning houses and earning money however she could, all the while keeping her own house clean and pretty. People still say, "She did it on a shoestring," when they talk about Elise Freidrich's pretty house, complimentary in their talk because they liked Elise and now they like remembering her.

You wouldn't know this unless you've lived in Hamburg for many years and maybe not even then, that Elise Freidrich was the person in town people quietly approached when they needed to talk. Elise was a loving caring listener who'd never-in-the-world repeat what they told her. She could've written a tell-all book but she wouldn't and people knew it. When she died a good share of the town turned out for the wake, and the funeral had to be held in the Hamburg Community Hall where there was enough seating for the mourners.

Eva and Dierdre were both like their mother, as in *hard worker* and *good manager*, and like their mother they both knew how to keep a secret.

Eva didn't have Dierdre's looks but Walter Hannamann, a serious young man, didn't seem to care. A year ahead of her in high school, he kept his eye on Eva and saw what boys caught up in the teen culture didn't see. He saw a serious girl doing her homework and studying for tests. A quiet girl who didn't sleep around. A sensible girl people trusted. Eva wanted to go to the state college and study to be a teacher but Walter knew he'd lose her if she went away. For himself, he had no eye for college. He wanted to farm the Hannamann land. Farming was what he was brought up to do and farming was what he wanted to do and he made up his mind he wanted Eva on the farm with him. So he courted her and won her, and they had a pretty early June wedding the month after she graduated.

Dierdre…another story. Unlike Eva who spent her time studying, Dierdre spent her time flirting with the boys and managed to get herself pregnant the last month of her senior year. The boy lived with his mother on the farm next to the Hannamann land and planned to farm it, just as Walter planned to farm his family's land. Dierdre and the boy got married that summer, lost the baby shortly after, and the boy's mother, Leah Bonhoff, died that summer, too. People said it was probably trauma that killed her, thinking about her darling boy marrying Dierdre Freidrich of all people, who was of the town poor and had a raging reputation at that. So the baby died and the mother-in-law died and wouldn't you know the boy got mad at Dierdre one day and left in a huff to join the army and got killed in a wild late-night car crash off the base.

Dierdre ended up with the farm. Just like that, practically overnight, by default Dierdre Freidrich became a landowner.

Dierdre, being Elise's daughter, a worker and a manager, was also savvy. To the surprise of the watching community the girl pulled things together and made a go of it on her farm. With stubborn diligence she did her own research on machinery and seeds and fertilizer and added to her knowledge by sorting through valuable information from a few of the neighboring farmers who couldn't resist having a young woman listener for their farming successes. It took some time to learn and she took some nasty falls, but being a worker and a manager and savvy, and now proving to be a trooper, she picked herself right up after every fall and went at it again. The first year or two people kept their eyes on her, sure she would fail. "Can you believe that Dierdre?" they'd say to each other with smug clicking tongues. "What does that crazy wild girl think she's doing?"

But Dierdre didn't fail. She kept right on trooping and people started slacking off on their snide remarks, reluctantly admitting the crazy wild girl, now a crazy wild woman, seemed to be making it work. Who would believe? But they still watched so they could gossip. It was petty none-of-their-business gossip like, "The woman hires out her work because she doesn't like to get her hands dirty. She likes to tear around in her little red convertible."

The community keeps Dierdre at arm's length as far as friendship is concerned. They still say Dierdre Freidrich, a town girl and a poor town girl with a bad reputation at that, shouldn't be a farmer. Especially she shouldn't be a farmer on their own established turf.

But in spite of the shunning, Dierdre Bonhoff keeps going. She maintains tight books and keeps her nose to the grindstone at the crunch times of planting and harvest, and every year she learns more and makes better decisions for her farm.

The first time Eva drove into her driveway Dierdre didn't know what to make of it. She watched the car pull in and stop, her thoughts flying as Eva walked up the sidewalk to ring the doorbell.

"There's word from Callie Sue and Eva's come to tell me."

"Eva's found out about Buck."

"Callie Sue came home." (Wouldn't it be nice if

Callie Sue came home? Oh, Lord, wouldn't it be nice if one day she just showed up?)

When Dierdre opened the door, though, she knew things were the same. Eva wore the same sad smile she'd worn like a mask every day since Callie Sue ran away.

"Thought I'd stop by with this kuchen I made. Thought you might have coffee on the stove," Eva said.

Dierdre stepped back. She'd see what this was all about, this visit from Eva, who hadn't come for such a long time.

They didn't talk about Callie Sue that first day. They talked about growing up in their pretty little house in Hamburg and about the mother they both loved and missed.

The next time Eva came they remembered school times and smiled at the memories. They remembered Eva's first grade teacher, Miss Jamison, who was too pretty and didn't last after her first year, and they remembered getting stranded overnight at the school in a snowstorm so severe they couldn't see a foot ahead to walk home.

On another visit Eva listened patiently when Dierdre broke down and cried about losing her baby that first summer out of high school.

Eva and Dierdre didn't talk about Callie Sue for

several visits.

When they did finally work up to Callie Sue, Dierdre told Eva how sorry she was she encouraged Callie Sue to be her own person, and if she could start over she wouldn't contribute to Callie Sue's rebellion. Eva told Dierdre that she, Eva, was responsible for Callie Sue running away. She nagged her to study more. The mother who hated competition nagged her own daughter to be competitive. And she didn't do what mothers are supposed to do, which is give unconditional love. Eva told Dierdre the two of them had trouble every day during that last tempestuous year Callie Sue was home.

On the day they finally talked about Callie Sue the sisters sat at Dierdre's kitchen table and sobbed. Tears ran down their faces like water let out of a dam. In their tearful confessions, though, the sisters weren't entirely honest. That is, if one can say omission is dishonesty. Remember, like their mother, Elise, they both knew how to keep a secret. Dierdre and Eva each kept a secret under lock and key that day at Dierdre's kitchen table.

Dierdre didn't tell Eva about Buck.

She wouldn't do it. She wouldn't open her can of worms to watch the biggest one crawl out and do its damage. To see the Hannamanns decry her even more than they already do and feel the rejection when the whole damned farming community, as a united force, maligns her and turns against her. Not that the community isn't already united against her, but it could be worse. Dierdre decided long ago that *Buck Whoever You Are* would remain her secret. On the confession day she was faithful to her decision.

Eva's secret was bigger. It was a humdinger of a secret. It was a humdinger of a secret she'd kept for many years and she wasn't about to tell it now.

Eva didn't tell Dierdre that Callie Sue isn't a Hannamann.

All along Callie Sue distinguished herself by not fitting into Hannamann ways and Eva, only Eva, knows the reason why. What she knows, that others don't know, is that Callie Sue has no Hannamann genes.

Eva didn't tell Dierdre there was a boy in her class who made her heart flutter every time she looked at him. A wild exciting boy. On the night of graduation when her cheeks were flushed with excitement and she wore her prettiest dress, the wild exciting boy looked her way and liked what he saw. She didn't tell Diedre that after that one magical night the boy looked elsewhere, no longer interested in Eva Freidrich. He had no idea that after their one night fling Eva Freidrich carried his child in her womb.

All these years Eva's kept her secret, never telling

one person. Not even Walter. Especially not Walter. He has no idea. She's sure he has no idea.

The secret only Eva knows will not be told. Not to Walter or to anyone else in the Hannamann family. Not even to Dierdre, her own sister.

Driving to Dierdre's farm this morning, with a bag of home-baked cookies on the seat beside her, Eva's surprised she feels halfway decent. She'd slept late, a surprise in itself, and when she finally opened her eyes to full sunlight streaming in the window she heard Walter downstairs making coffee.

He brought a hot steaming cup upstairs on a tray, along with toast and orange juice, smiling and happy with himself for doing something nice for her. He sat by her bed while she ate, talking to her about the crops and the weather and then, surprise of all surprises, he wondered if they should drive to Gutenburg in the afternoon to have dinner and take in a play.

As Eva drives to Dierdre's the sun's still shining and the day is pleasantly warm and balmy. She hopes the sun is shining on her darling Callie Sue. Wherever she is. She hopes her darling Callie Sue is basking in the sun's warm rays. Wherever she is.

Looking forward to seeing her sister, Eva turns into Dierdre's driveway. Dierdre will meet her at the door dressed in one of her ruffled short skirts and she'll be wearing strappy shoes. She'll be smiling. She'll open her arms and they'll hug each other tightly.

"Come in and have coffee," Dierdre will say. "I've been waiting for you. I'm so glad you're here."

The Little Brother

Through the Years

"A pleasant illusion is better than a harsh reality."
— *Christian Nestell Bovee*
American Writer

Little Otto, early on shortened to L.O. and later to just Lo, is the baby of the Hannamann family. He's a docile child, not confrontational in the least. He doesn't break rules.

A relief after Callie Sue's rampages.

When Eva and Walter sit on the porch talking in the evenings Lo is there listening, liking the companionship and finding great satisfaction in being with his parents. More than anything he likes to tag along with Walter in the fields. When he helps his dad his reward is, "Good job, Lo." He beams and works all the harder for favor.

Five years old when Callie Sue ran away.

Lo doesn't talk about the very bad day. No one talks about it. But Callie Sue's in his head all of the time. She doesn't pop into his thoughts only at certain times, like when he sees someone smile like Callie Sue smiled, sudden happiness lighting up her face. Or when he sees a red stocking cap like Callie Sue's red stocking cap, bouncing around on someone else's head. It isn't just an occasional glimmer of memory.

Not like that. Like I say, Callie Sue's with Lo all of the time, a constant companion. She sits with him in his room when he does his homework. She sits with him on the school bus to Hamburg and even goes into his classrooms with him. Callie Sue talks to Lo and he talks to her. Callie Sue's his best friend. She's also his only friend.

Walter and Eva have no idea. Walter and Eva think their son is naturally quiet and contented, not needing to seek out friends. There are children like this. And after all, Walter was a quiet homebody when he was growing up and he's still a quiet homebody. Lo takes after Walter.

Five years old when Dad took the truck out looking for Callie Sue.

When Lo woke up that morning Dad was gone, and Mother said he was out looking for Callie Sue because she didn't come home last night. Then Uncle Earle showed up in his cruiser, this time not interested in taking him out for a ride. Instead, Uncle Earle sat at the kitchen table talking to Mother, drinking Mother's coffee. Lo was there in the kitchen too, sitting by himself nibbling on cinnamon toast and sipping orange juice, making it last a long time so he could listen in. He heard it all. He heard Uncle Earle tell Mother, "Callie Sue ran away. Don't worry. She'll be back soon."

Five years old when Callie Sue didn't run away.

On the very day Uncle Earle sat in the kitchen with Mother, Callie Sue moved in with him. She sat at the end of his bed when he went back to his room after breakfast. "Little Otto," she said. "I'm here." She went on. "I'm going to stay here with you. We don't need to tell anyone. It'll be our secret." He'll always remember her next words. "Little Otto, I haven't left you. I could never leave you. I'll always be here for you."

So far Callie Sue hasn't failed him and Lo is depending on her to stay. He doesn't think his sister will let him down.

Seven years old when Lo found Callie Sue's locket.

He went with Dad to Grandmother Lily's empty house when he checked to see if the water pipes were holding up, to make sure the lock on the front door was intact, to walk through the rooms to see that everything was in order. When Dad was upstairs looking around Lo checked out the cubbyhole in Grandmother's dresser where he and Anna and Callie Sue hid things. And there it was. Callie Sue's locket. Right there in the cubbyhole, almost as though she knew he'd find it.

He quickly picked it up and put it in his pocket. "Callie Sue," he said, "I found your locket." At home he opened it and there was his photo on one side and Anna's on the other.

He hid the locket in the treasure box he keeps at the back of his own dresser drawer.

The years go by, and every so often he pulls it out of the box and looks at it. Lo doesn't tell anyone he has the locket. It's his secret and Callie Sue's secret.

The Real Story

Callie Sue Hannamann

Ozella

The Runaway

Six Years Later
2003

"What is called resignation is
confirmed desperation."
— *Henry David Thoreau*

Callie Sue Hannamann stood at the large window in the living room of the California condo. She watched the waves of the Pacific Ocean pounding in, breaking onto the rocks below and sending huge sprays of water into the air when they hit. She followed the waves as they washed in, liking their steady beat. Predictable and dependable, never rushing and never delaying. Always the same.

"Something to be said for always the same," she sighed. "When I was fourteen you couldn't tell me 'always the same' was a good thing."

The late afternoon sun showered the incoming waves with slanting rays of light, showing off a brilliant kaleidoscope of color on the beads of water spraying into the air.

Watching the pounding waves and the sun's rays on the water did nothing to ease Callie Sue's restless day. It started early in the day... the restlessness, the aimless wandering and lack of focus. Now, in the afternoon, she's at the window taking stock of her life. She's looking back, pondering, and sorting out the good from the bad.

The sorting isn't going well.

"Not going well because sorting's a child's game," she decided. "Sorting's too simple. I'm not a child and my life isn't simple. I'm a twenty-year-old woman coping with a complicated dangerous life, often teetering on the brink of existence. I shouldn't allow myself to play the simple games of children. My game has to be serious calculating with the goal of staying alive."

Callie Sue's a beautiful young woman and she knows she must stay beautiful. No drugs for her. No alcohol allowed except when working, and then only minimum indulgence. No smoking. Slim because she keeps herself slim. Her job *(*Job? She laughs bitterly.) demands beauty. It demands chic style, too. Stunning designer clothes hang in the walk-in closet of the condo and Ozella takes her to the nicest stores to shop for cosmetics. He insists on professional styling for her hair, having no problem paying expensive stylists for their services.

"Is this the good?" Callie Sue asks herself as she looks for a dangling thread of decency to hang on to.

Today it's hard to hang on to anything, even on what she tentatively labels good. It has turned out to be a wretched day, tainted with unwanted painful memories. Usually she manages to keep the memories at bay but today they're slipping in.

The sun's glow on the water has something to do

with it. She should know better than to stand at this window. She's been mesmerized here before by the sun's rays playing on the waves, enticing her to let down her guard and teasing her into false security. The deceptive scene says, "Everything's good, Callie Sue. Don't worry about a thing." To that foolish head-in-the-sand thinking Grandmother Lily would have said, "Rubbish," and Callie Sue agrees. Everything isn't good and she's well-aware the fickle and elusive *everything's good* can change to *everything's bad* on the turn of a dime.

Six years since the August day she disappeared from Hannamann Farms. No longer the impetuous young girl doing her best to break rein from playing the role of a proper Hannamann. No longer the innocent pretty girl born into a family living by well-established habits and set-in-stone expectations, leaving little room for deviation.

When she didn't come home to Hannamann Farms that afternoon six years ago, Aunt Dierdre would've spilled the beans about Buck. They'd all decide right then and there she ran away. Usually the Hannamanns get one thought in their heads and there it stays, rolling around collecting believability. It seeps into all the little nooks and crannies, filling their brains to capacity, and from that time on they declare with intractable sureness to themselves and to the world, "This is the way it is." Callie Sue is guessing her family's, "This is the way it is," was "Callie Sue ran away."

Only they got it wrong. Hopelessly wrong.

It was August, the month before the start of school, the month of the State Fair, the month of hot days when the corn matures and the ears on the stalks fill out with kernels. The waiting month on the farm, some people say. Waiting for summer to be over, waiting for school to start, waiting for cooler weather, waiting for the first days of harvest. "The month they were sure I ran away," Callie Sue mused.

She cringed, knowing full well what's coming next. She's been here before.

When she's so careless to let down her guard, like right now, the Dreaded Question shows up. It blinks like an insistent alarm, not to be denied. It sends in waves of self-doubt and puts a mean-spirited dent in the little confidence she has left.

The Dreaded Question: *"Why didn't they find me?"*

And lately more nagging questions showing up, propping up the big one.

"Were they embarrassed about me back then?"

"If I ran away was I out of sight? Out of mind?"

"Did believing I ran away solve their dilemma of what to do about Callie Sue?"

It hurts so much, this wondering why her family didn't find her, and now wondering if they even tried to find her.

And always wondering, always and forever wondering, if they found her locket. She'd thought carefully where to hide it. When Martine slipped up one day and left the room she hobbled to Grandmother's dresser and put it in the little cubbyhole behind one of the drawers. She and Anna and Little Otto hid treasures there when they played at Grandmother's house.

Hopefully, when Anna and Little Otto come to the house they'll check out the cubbyhole and find her locket. And finding it will lead to questions. "Why is Callie Sue's locket here? How did it get here?"

Surely Anna or Little Otto would find the locket. Dear God, how could they not find it?

She knows now, though, after six years, that her wonderings do no good. It's wasted energy because she can't go back to Hannamann Farms anyhow, even if the locket is found. Ozella will come for her if she leaves, and even if he doesn't come (but he will) she'll always carry an impossible burden. "I'm used merchandise now. I'm damaged used merchandise and my family couldn't accept it. They'd take me in and try to understand but their shame would eventually win out."

"What do we tell the neighbors?" they'd ask. Or, "Is it not Callie Sue's own fault she's where she is?" And the eventual, the unthinkable, "Wouldn't it be better for everyone if Callie Sue hadn't come back?"

It isn't hard to figure out she's blackened the Hannamann reputation. Even if she simply ran away like she told Aunt Diedre she'd do, her family's admired standing in the community would be tarnished. Once shining silver, now tarnished with an ugly blemish.

In the last years Callie Sue's come to terms with not going home to Hannamann Farms, a dream she kept alive at first. Now she tries not to think about Mother and her dad, and Anna and Little Otto. She won't be visiting Grandmother Lily in her pretty apartment at Quiet Haven either. And she won't be helping her dad at harvest time, the only job on the farm she liked. Her dad always said, "Don't know what I'd do without you, Callie Sue. You're the best help I have."

In the first terrible years she cried for her mother every night, dreaming of her mother taking her in her arms, holding her close and stroking her back. She dreamed of her mother gently brushing away her tears of shame.

Mostly she dreamed of her mother's forgiveness.

Unable to hold back tears, Callie Sue moved away

from the window, away from the pounding waves and spraying water. She walked to the couch and fluffed the pillows to lie down. Just a few minutes of rest and then up to get ready for her appointment.

"It's true I wanted to leave Hannamann Farms," she thought as she put her head on the pillow. It was August and how well she remembers her yearnings to run away. More than anything she wanted to escape. To not go back to school to boring classes and the drudgery of hated homework, and all the while listening at home to the predictable nagging of her mother to study more and get good grades.

"If you spend more time studying, Callie Sue, you can have good grades like Anna's." An intolerable never-ending warped record from her mother, who had somehow changed from a warm loving mother to a cold, pushy and unyielding *frumpy* mother she couldn't identify with.

Studying more wasn't to be. Instead of heeding her mother's badgering to study she yearned for another life. She even made up a story one day when she was at Aunt Diedre's about a man named Buck. Buck would take her away and together they'd roam the world, far away from Hannamann constraints. Aunt Dierdre bought her story lock, stock, and barrel. She actually relished the story and encouraged Callie Sue to tell her more.

Curiously though, Aunt Dierdre didn't ask even one time, "Buck who?"

"Hey, Callie Sue, can I give you a lift?"

It was Jacobs, the man her dad rented Grandmother Lily's farmhouse to when she moved to Quiet Haven. He stopped his pickup truck on the blacktop road where she was walking to Aunt Dierdre's farm, a mile away. Aunt Dierdre didn't know she was coming but she was always welcome. "Come any time, Callie Sue," Aunt Dierdre always said.

"No thanks. I like to walk and this is such a nice day to be out," Callie Sue answered as she waved Jacobs on. He waved too and drove on, but a short way down the road he stopped the truck and backed it up.

"Callie Sue," he called from the open window. "We found some jewelry your grandmother left behind. A necklace and a couple of rings." He looked up and down the road before going on. "You could stop over and pick them up for her and I'll bring you back. Martine's on my case to get them returned."

Callie Sue didn't want to go right then.

I have plans. I know the man. He's been around all summer and helps my dad sometimes. My dad says Jacobs has a mechanical mind with machinery and he's glad to have him here now when he's getting the machinery ready for harvest. It's all right to climb in the truck with him but I don't want to give up my time right now.

But even with this reluctance Callie Sue climbed up into the cab of the truck. Her thought was, "Why not. I'll be on my way soon."

Jacobs drove fast, which suited her fine, and pulled up to Grandmother Lily's house. Callie Sue always liked seeing it and now remembered the many times her family came to the house for Sunday dinner or a birthday celebration, or stopped by when they were out for an evening drive looking at the crops. Sometimes on hot summer nights Grandfather Otto got out his old crank ice cream maker and Grandmother Lily called them to come for homemade ice cream.

Callie Sue opened the door of the truck, climbed down, and started for the door half-expecting Grandmother Lily to open it and throw her arms wide for the first hug. It wasn't Grandmother Lily at the door, though. The woman, Martine, opened it, and she looked at Jacobs with curious questioning eyes that asked, "What's this?" Jacobs nodded to her. Callie Sue walked through the open doorway.

Her stomach turned as she remembers what happened next.

From behind, Jacobs grabbed her arms and held them back. Martine ran for a kitchen towel and wound it around her head into a blindfold, and they pushed Callie Sue across the kitchen to the living room and on into the first-floor bedroom where Grandmother and Grandfather always slept. Jacobs' hand was over her mouth. She can feel it even now, his big hand on her mouth, and she can still feel the choking when she couldn't shout out or scream because the hand was clamped on tight. She remembers Jacobs saying to Martine, "We've got her. It was so easy. The girl is so stupid."

The 'what happened next'…was Jacobs did the unspeakable. Are you ready for this? Jacobs, the quiet unassuming man her dad rented Grandmother Lily's house to, raped Callie Sue.

In one despicable and heinous act, right there on the bed in Grandmother Lily's bedroom, Jacobs brutally raped our innocent and unsuspecting fourteen-year-old Callie Sue Hannamann. A planned act of violence. He'd been watching. He'd been watching for his opportunity, and opportunity fell in his lap.

It was so easy.

When Callie Sue was secured Martine took off the makeshift towel blindfold and left the room. They wanted her to see the whole thing. They wanted her to hear the sick laughter of Jacobs. They wanted her to feel the pain.

They especially wanted her to be left with shame. In that quest they were successful.

In that one despicable and heinous act, right there on the bed in Grandmother Lily's bedroom, Jacobs gave Callie Sue the shame he wanted her to have. It wasn't shallow shame to be casually tossed off, but deep-seated imbedded shame that hung around and hung around, slyly lurking under the surface of life, always ready to rise to the top.

It was a devastating exchange. Jacobs, with planned carnal lust took Callie Sue's spontaneity, her pride, her confidence, her excitement for living. He took it all, and more, and when he finished taking he replaced what he'd taken with just one thing. He replaced it with Deep Shame.

It settled in quietly and surreptitiously, like heavy fog settles in in the dark of night. Callie Sue didn't see the shame at first, or feel its heavy weight, because she was frightened and being frightened took up all the space in her head right then. No matter. She absorbed the shame like a sponge absorbs water, soaking it up as storage.

And just as a sponge filled with water is heavy, the sponge filled with shame was heavy. Later, Callie

Sue tried many times to wring it out or shake it off, but she couldn't because it was in her now. The heavy torturous shame took up residence and became a part of her being.

When it was over Martine came back. She and Jacobs gagged her and left her sobbing on the bed. Just as they planned, the memory of Jacobs coming toward her in the bedroom would stay with her forever, the sound of his sick laughter was etched in her brain, she would always hurt from the pain they wanted her to feel, and Deep Shame would always be imbedded within.

In the morning she was still there. She heard a car drive up the lane and her dad asked Jacobs at the door if they'd seen anything of Callie Sue because she didn't come home last night and they were worried. Still tied down on Grandmother's bed with the gag in her mouth, with Martine in the corner of the room pointing a gun at her, she heard Jacobs say, with concern in his voice, "I'm sorry there's a problem. I'm going into town later. I'll ask around."

Jacobs and Martine worked together that morning to clean her up and get her dressed. Then they gave her cold cereal at the kitchen table, all the while with her feet tied. Jacobs aimed the gun at her when she tried to eat, when she gagged on the cereal, and said, "Callie Sue, if you scream or make any noise I'll shoot you." As simple as that. "I'll shoot you," he said. She remembers his voice was quiet and smooth, like calm water without a ripple.

Callie Sue had no doubt he'd do it. He'd shoot her and bury her in a deep grave in the cornfield and not one other person except Martine would ever know.

Then Jacobs and Martine did another unspeakable and unimaginable thing, and they managed to pull it off. They kept Callie Sue in Grandmother Lily's house. Right there in her house, right there on Hannamann property, right there under unsuspecting Hannamann noses. The gun was always in Jacobs' or Martine's hand when she wasn't secured and gagged.

She sobbed and pleaded. She tried to keep track of time as days faded into nights and nights slipped into days, but her mind was muddled and she couldn't keep time straight. And all the while she was muddled Jacobs had his way with her, each time diminishing her more.

She didn't know what was going to happen next. After a while she didn't care what happened next. Probably Jacobs would finally shoot her and he and Martine would bury her, and she hoped it would be soon. She stopped eating. She prayed for sleep. When she finally slept she woke up crying.

One day she was aware Jacobs and Martine were

packing. In the middle of that night they piled her into the truck along with their clothes and dishes and the rest of their belongings, and like a hated snake that's just satisfied its appetite on prey and is heading out, the truck slithered down the curving gravel lane to the blacktop road and headed out.

Under blankets in the back of the cab, securely bound and gagged, Callie Sue remembered Jacobs' words to Martine. "We've got her. It was so easy. The girl is so stupid."

The telephone buzzed. Callie Sue reached for it on the cocktail table and answered. "This is Caroline," she said. The voice at the other end was expected. She listened to the usual arrangements.

She put the phone down and leaned back on the pillow, shaken now from the vivid memories. How does an innocent fourteen-year-old farm girl, a child really, live with rape and kidnapping and the sordid life she was pitched into? More than once in the last six years she's plotted to check out. A final way to escape the dishonor and shame of what she's doing.

Sobbing now, angry, she pushed herself up as she tried to find pardon, foraging in the raw painful memories in search of a defense to shore up her credit.

But I didn't check out, did I? I didn't kill myself. I was strong.

I survived.

That night I survived the drive to Chicago in the cab of the truck, and I survived the next drive to California in the back of the panel truck. And once in California I survived the beatings from Ozella.

Ozella…the name that still makes her cringe in fear and shrink back, waiting for blows.

Ozella…the out-of-control abuser who went too far one day when he beat a girl, and the girl died. That day she, Callie Sue, screamed at Ozella to stop. "Stop it, you brute," coming out of her mouth without thinking, while beating on him with her fists and crying out for the girl to run.

And then Ozella struck *her* to the floor. "Get out of my way, bitch, or you'll be next."

Ozella…the buyer component in an evil business transaction. Jacobs and Martine the sellers. Ozella the buyer and Callie Sue the commodity. The human commodity. The 'hot goods' commodity, carefully smuggled across the country.

The day after she was sold to Ozella in California he put her in a room, alone with him, and proceeded to beat her. "Teaching you a lesson," he said.

"What lesson?" she wondered. "What lesson am

I supposed to learn?" For a girl who had never been hit, being purposely hurt with well-aimed blows was incomprehensible. Only later did she figure out the beating served an important purpose for Ozella. He was diminishing her, making her more pliable. First the rapes, then the raw savage beating. And afterward Ozella threatening daily, sometimes hourly, "There's more where that came from."

A terrible time for fourteen-year-old Callie Sue Hannamann.

Ozella delivered on his threat. He beat her two more times. Again, the beatings were violent and severe, the last one when she had a scheme to run away and Ozella found out, so severe she barely hung on. His final number on her. His deadly warning to never again get it in her head to run.

"Girl, you are one dead bitch if you run. I'll find you." He was shouting, out of control. "I'll come after you and find you wherever you are. You believe it, girl. This is the way it works."

Callie Sue backed away from Ozella, shielding her head from the coming blows as he charged at her with rage. He was shouting and spewing out damning expletives and threats like a savage bellowing animal on the rampage. Grabbing Callie Sue's shoulders, he shook her hard and made her look him in the eye. Then, gripping her arm with one fist he gave her hard bruising jabs with the other, going for her ribs instead of her head. A hard bruising jab every time he spit out a threat. She doubled over in pain, fearing for her life.

"You think I don't know where you come from?" Ozella shouted. "You think I don't know about your stupid farm and your idiot family? I'll find them and kill them all before I kill you and I'll make you watch. By God, I'll make you watch. I swear to God I'll make you watch your family dying."

Finally, as she sobbed and begged for mercy, Ozella threw her to the floor and gave her a last hard kick. "Get it through your thick little farm girl head you belong to me. You try running away you f-----g won't live to tell it and your family won't either. You hear?"

I heard.

I heard, even using every scrap of energy I had trying to live through the beating. Ozella knew where I came from and he knew about my family. He'd search out Mother and my dad and Anna and Little Otto and kill them, and then he'd kill me. I heard it all and I got it. He'd do it. Even early on I figured out Ozella makes good on his threats.

That day was the end for me. I didn't mess up again. From then on, instead of foolishly putting my efforts into schemes to go home, I put my efforts into staying alive and keeping my family alive. I wised up and did what I had to do. From that day on I was one of Ozella's willing prostitutes, out on the streets turning tricks for him. I was the world's best-programmed robot, blindly obeying and following every rule.

I never again questioned Ozella's authority. Never again did I give him cause to think I'd do anything else but follow his rules. And especially never again did I give him cause to think I'd run.

I stuck with my goal. With an "X" only I knew the meaning of, I marked on my calendar each day I was still alive. I settled into a dull calm, marking off days while trying not to do anything stupid. Trying to stay alive. Trying to keep my family alive.

Drained now, depleted in energy and confidence, deep in misery, Callie Sue struggled to feel better.

I'm still alive. There's that. Staying alive and keeping my family alive counts for something.

And I'm in a better place now.

You, who haven't been in my shoes, won't agree, saying it doesn't matter if you're a low-end street walker or a high-end escort. You're still a prostitute. "The precise label doesn't matter," you'll say. "What matters is what you are, and what you are now is a high-end escort prostitute."

What you mean, I think, is, "What you are now is a high-end escort slut."

But how would you know? How can you judge? You

aren't in my shoes.

Callie Sue pulled herself up and walked back to the window. She watched the waves still crashing in, still steady and strong. A reminder to stay the course and be strong? Their steadiness and predictable sureness a dependable thread to hang on to? She knows she's reaching. One more time reaching and probing and sifting through her pitiful life for something…anything…to make it better.

"Dear God, are there *any* threads for me to grasp?" she whispered. "Will there ever be?" With sagging shoulders and tears still in her eyes she added, " I have so little to hang on to."

Standing at the window tired and miserable and wishing things were different, knowing things weren't going to be different, Callie Sue forced herself back to the reality she hates. "This is where I am and this is what I am," she told herself. "I have nowhere else to go. Other girls go home. Other girls aren't prostitutes."

Brushing back the last of her tears, Callie Sue turned from the pounding waves and the deceptive rays of the sun on the water. "Time to stop this and get on with my disgraceful wretched life," she told herself with resignation. It was the resignation, and desperation, of a beaten down, nowhere to go, pitifully exploited victim of human bondage.

And so it was, that on the late afternoon of her unsettling day of unrest and miserable memories, Callie Sue Hannamann one more time came to the brutal truth of her reality. "I'm a prostitute, and this is my life."

She pulled herself together then and slowly walked to the bedroom of Ozella's California condo, where she would prepare for her client.

The Criminal

Shrewd and Polished
Arrogant
Hardcore Criminal Mind

"I never wonder to see men
wicked, but I often wonder
to see them not ashamed."
– Jonathan Swift

Early on Callie Sue senses Ozella favors her and she's right. He does favor her. She's younger than his other girls but already has the figure men like, and good healthy skin, and strong shapely legs that can't be better in the stiletto heels he demands. He's careful with her, and watchful. Took care not to leave scars when he beat her, and now keeps a vigilant eye on her clientele.

He sets the stage early for what he has in mind.

In his business beauty counts big. Callie Sue more than meets that requirement. But the stubborn determination she wears like a badge also counts as a strong point, even if keeping her in line means strong threats and never-ending intimidation. And Ozella notices that Callie Sue, unlike his other girls, measures every situation. She doesn't just observe. She measures. She's like a ruthless calculating cat assessing each situation before her. All the above good for work on the streets.

All the above good for more than work on the streets.

The girl has something else he doesn't exactly understand but it's there. Callie Sue's good with his girls. They like her and trust her, and when there's trouble she offers them kindness. Kindness is new territory for Ozella. In his evil world, coming across an innately kind person is rare. He wonders how it is that a person can be both ruthless and kind. He wonders if the strange pairing of *ruthless* and *kind* will be an asset or a problem.

For this unique young girl, this beautiful unique young girl who's head and shoulders above his other girls, he has a big plan. He doesn't want problems, even small problems. Small problems lead to big problems and big problems lead to trouble.

He plans carefully and shrewdly. With crafty cunning, always watching, never letting up on threats and always keeping Callie Sue on edge, Ozella grooms her for big money. Only the best for this girl. Nothing trashy or cheap. He takes her to top-of-the-line hair stylists and makeup artists and buys her expensive tasteful fashions from smart boutiques.

They frequent pricey restaurants where he teaches Callie Sue to sit properly and eat properly. Where he teaches her to look at him with adoring eyes.

His elite clientele will appreciate adoring eyes. They'll be pleased. They'll call back.

Now he's delighted, savoring his cleverness like the cat that ate the canary, when a buyer asks for Callie Sue. He offers her with sly reluctance, dragging his feet on the deal. He gets his voice down soft, dripping with serious intent, and taking his time reminds the buyer of Callie Sue's desirability. "You're asking for the best, you know. You're asking for the cream of the crop."

The selling price is high and goes up for each repeat call. Callie Sue Hannamann, known only as 'Caroline', on call-backs commands three thousand a night, minimum. On a first call no less than two.

Who knows what he can get in the future? Maybe double.

A man of nefarious intent and insatiable greed, Ozella's shameless mind works overtime. Contemplating his next move, he smiles because the scene is set. No doubt about it. Human trafficking is lucrative and growing and he has one Callie Sue Hannamann (now, thanks to his savvy, the beautiful and desirable 'Caroline') ready to make unlimited money for him.

And he hasn't even started tapping into sports events where the big spenders show up.

Soon now. Very soon now.

A New Chapter

Super Bowl XXXVII

San Diego, CA
January 26, 2003

"New sexy & beautiful girls in town, waiting for u."

*Ad posted on the Internet
before a Super Bowl*

When one of his grandchildren, one of us, did a badness, Grandfather Betz liked to say, "What goes around comes around." With a knowing gleam in his eye he warned, "Be careful. You can get your badness back, right in your face."

If he were here today Grandfather would remind us that Ozella got his badness back, and right in his face, too. "Told you it can happen," he would say.

As was his plan, Ozella took Callie Sue to a sports event, the first of many he thought. With a beginner's naïve anticipation of success coupled with his inflated ego, he chose big…the Super Bowl hosted that year in California. In his excitement he even imagined the new venture was destiny. "Why, it's meant to be," he told himself when he heard the Super Bowl was to be in nearby San Diego. "I've been thinking about this for a long time. I'm ready and Callie Sue's ready. The Super Bowl showing up here in California, right now at this time, is a positive sign."

But a positive sign it was not, and in fact turned out to be Ozella's undoing. Always before a careful shrewd planner, proud he didn't make mistakes, this time he erred. Overestimating his savvy and arriving in San

Diego with Callie Sue to a complex world he thought he understood but didn't, Ozella failed to take into account the well organized vice squad agents roaming sports venues looking for his kind. Particularly roaming Super Bowl venues.

Arrest was waiting to happen. The hardcore criminal, so sure he had a good thing going, was quickly arrested and taken off the streets. Almost in the blink of an eye he traded places with Callie Sue. Callie Sue in bondage one day and free the next. Ozella free one day and in bondage the next.

I ask you, "How great is that? Are we complaining? Are you there, Grandfather Betz?"

So now, in the wake of this unexpected turn of events, Callie Sue's story changes. Everything about her story changes. Before Ozella's arrest a puppet manipulated on a string by her captor. After his arrest an abandoned hanging puppet, left dangling to find her own way.

Suddenly Callie Sue's in unfamiliar territory. Ozella's gone, she's hanging alone, and how will she do this? How will she untangle the strings and navigate the unknown? Six years of living in bondage offered no lessons on how to live without constraints. This is new territory, and it's terrifying.

We, the naïve, breathe a sigh of relief. Now Callie Sue can have the privileges of freedom we love. We have choices and now she can have choices. We have dreams for the future and now she can have goals and dreams for the future. We eagerly anticipate a new life for Callie Sue. "She's paid her dues. She deserves it," we say.

Not so fast. Don't be so sure. Even if Callie Sue has paid her dues and deserves a new life, the new life won't be laid out on a silver platter. New challenges await and they won't be easy to conquer.

Callie Sue's first challenge is jail. She spends her first night of freedom from bondage in the San Diego Municipal Jail, where she's sat down at a steel table in a cold room and drilled for hours with probing questions. She's the recipient of the demeaning disrespect reserved for prostitutes. She's leered at with scorn, eyed with disgust, and automatically pitched into the category of second-class citizen. Or third-class citizen.

Tired and frightened after the long night of interrogation, sure she's in for a long jail sentence, Callie Sue's surprised to be released the next morning. "A first offense here," the booking officer reports. "Nothing in the records to say this one's been here before."

So after more paperwork and more scorn, Callie Sue's released. On the way out she's warned by a preachy officer she'd better not be picked up again. Next time she'll have an extended stay, she can count on it, and does she understand this is the way the system works? Because the system's tired of the likes of her messing up their city. No siree, she won't be so lucky if he sees her again. Does she get it? She'd better get it.

Callie Sue's meek reply is what we'd expect from a person coming off six years of forced bondage. Frightened, with proper subservience and eyes looking down she whispers, " Yes, sir. I get it, sir." Then, afraid of the officer and thinking he might change his mind and keep her in jail, she hurries to the door, pulls it open and quickly slips out. She dares not look back.

When Callie Sue walked out of the police station that morning, alone, she walked into a new world. What to do? Where to go? What next? One thing was sure. There were no loved ones with outstretched arms waiting at the curb to advise her or show her the way. Standing by herself on the sidewalk outside the door of the station, stunned, Callie Sue didn't have a clue of what to do or where to go. All she knew was she couldn't stay where she was, so she turned and walked away from the station as fast as she could. And once she started walking she didn't stop. She crossed street after street and turned corner after corner, blindly charging ahead with no idea where she was.

After some time, though, her walking slowed. At first the goal was to get away fast. But when she thought she was a safe distance away from the station she slowed her pace and began to look around.

When she came on a coffee shop with people milling around inside she went in, albeit with wariness, and sat in a booth and ordered coffee and a bagel. After the sleepless night in the jail and then frantically walking the streets to get away from the jail, she was dreadfully tired.

For a long time she sat in the booth biding time and resting, nibbling on the bagel and drinking her coffee. She watched the people around her as they went about their business. Ordinary people coming and going. Relaxed and busy people with seemingly important missions. Looking happy. Casual happy, like it's the most natural thing in the world to come into a shop and order coffee. "I'll have a latte," or "Just a cup of decaf today," they breezily announce as they smile at the server. .

When she ordered her own coffee and bagel she didn't (couldn't) look at the server, and smiling and breezily announcing anything was out of the question.

She was uncomfortable and felt out of place in the coffee shop. She didn't fit in. It occurred to her that maybe she wouldn't fit in anywhere. "I'm an outsider here," she told herself. "Maybe I'll be an outsider everywhere."

This sobering thought brought tears, reminding Callie Sue she's sitting in a booth by herself in a coffee shop moping and feeling sorry for herself. Reminding her she's not like these people who have lives and have coffee with friends and breezily announce things. Reminding her she *doesn't* have a life, and for sure she doesn't have friends, and it's pretty obvious she has to get busy and figure out what to do about it. She has to face reality. She has to work out a plan.

She went to get a refill of coffee then, and settled in to take stock of her situation. To see where she is. To start on a plan.

In making her assessment Callie Sue is honest, finding much not to like. She doesn't think she can go home. Going home isn't an option. So she has no family, no job, nowhere to live, and no friends to call. Now she's picked up a police record for prostitution. She thinks she might find a help agency but cancels the idea, leery of going down that path. After the shabby treatment at the jail her trust level is at an all-time low. She has no intention of putting herself out there again, answering more questions and spilling out details about her shameful life. There has to be a better way. She does have some money she's secretly squirrelled away through the years.

Tips from clients, carefully saved for her getaway dream and always hidden on her person. Having a little money is the only positive she can think of but even that has a negative side. There's not very much, and it won't last long.

Callie Sue wonders what's happening with Ozella. She thinks it isn't likely he'll be released, but if he is released he'll try to find her. Can she find a cheap hotel where she'll be anonymous? Where she can get off the streets for a while and be safe? Where she can rest and think things through? It would be temporary, but it would be a start.

She decided her first order of business would be to find such a hotel. She'd check out the Yellow Pages and discreetly ask questions, and it wouldn't be a bad thing to do some praying either. God hadn't done much for her in the years of bondage but he'd suddenly come through now in a big way.

"Dear God, please help me find a hotel," she silently prayed. "I need some help here." Whether it was God or her cautious savvy or just plain luck or all of the above, Callie Sue did find a cheap but decent hotel. She found it that very day. She was at the beginning of a plan.

Checking in as 'Susan Galvin' (where did she come up with that name?) she couldn't believe the relief of having four secure walls and her own key and a security lock on the door. Exhausted, at the end of her energy, she slept. She sank into deep sleep, far away from the horrors of bondage and far away from the freedom that would be her new reality.

As Callie Sue settled into the hotel in the next days she felt reasonably safe. But never once did she let down her guard when she was out and about. She kept a constant vigil for Ozella. A couple of times she thought (maybe imagined) she spied him in the distance, and rushed back to the safety of her room where she stayed for hours.

Even though Callie Sue felt reasonably safe in the hotel and was cautious outside, the rest she craved to clear her head wasn't forthcoming. Thinking things through didn't go well either. She tried to plan but nights brought unspeakable memories, and during the days she couldn't seem to get herself together. After a confidence day she invariably sank back into despair the next day. Dazed and confused and without direction she was like a bobber on rough water, flailing up and down and every which way.

We the unknowing, the unschooled in the dark side of life, have advice. That is to say, we have unasked-for advice regarding something we know nothing about.

Callie Sue should come home. She should come home to Hannamann Farms and live the life she lived before. (Why *doesn't* she come home?) "Come on home, little girl. You're free as a bird so wing your way back."

But living with Deep Shame and believing she's forever marked, the bewildered little girl asks, "Home? How can I go home?" And she wrestles with an even bigger dilemma. After not being found by her family and not sure of her standing at Hannamann Farms she wonders, "Do I still have a home?"

As Callie Sue battled despair and indecision in California, life back at Hannamann Farms plodded on, which is to say life went on as usual. No indecision here. Every day the family followed its routine of eating breakfast together before Anna and Lo left on the bus for school. Then Walter and Eva went about the business of managing Hannamann Farms, right now planning ahead for crops and getting ready for spring planting, which is what farm families do in late winter and early spring.

With all comfortably steady and on schedule, the family has no idea the call they've waited for, for years, is about to come.

It came in late March when Hannamann Farms was waking up from a long cold winter, not unlike the long cold winter the year before they lost Callie Sue. It came early in the morning on another routine day, a business as usual day when Walter would work on farm records in his office and there was Eva, sweet diligent Eva, hurrying with her kitchen chores so she could get out to uncover her gardens before the early shoots of spring bulbs showed up. It came as the family sat down to her bacon and eggs, in the silence just after Walter blessed the food and asked God's favor on Callie Sue. "Bless this food for our use," he prayed as heads bowed and hands clasped, "and we ask you to watch over our Callie Sue, wherever she may be."

A loud ring of the telephone broke into the quiet of the kitchen. It was sudden. It was also annoying. It was an intrusion into well-established Hannamann morning routine.

Eva went to answer.

"Hello," she said in an inconvenienced rude voice, which is not at all the way she usually answers the telephone. How regrettable that on this chance day in late March, answering this particular telephone call, Eva was rude.

No one answered.

She tried again and waited. "Hello?"

Eva was put off and cross because the call was

indeed an annoying intrusion. She had work to do. Her garden was waiting. At the very least the caller could favor her with a simple reply.

She was about to give it up when a faraway woman's voice said, "Hello? Hello, Mother?"

Eva gasped. Her hand went to her throat.

"Mother?"

The voice, meek and hesitant, asked again, "Are you there, Mother?"

Eva looked at Walter in panic, eyes filling with tears, and Walter looked back at his wife. *Dear God. He knew*. Pushing away from the table, he was across the room in an instant to Eva, folding her into his arms.

Another pause, this one long, before the long-awaited-for and never-to-be-forgotten words spilled out.

"Mother," the voice said as it broke into a sob. "It's me. It's me, Callie Sue . . ."

Late Spring, 2003

"He that is without sin among you,
let him first cast a stone at her."
John 8:7

It was on one of her better days, a confidence day, when Callie Sue worked herself up to making the telephone call. Before this day, every time she considered going home her lonesome yearning competed with Deep Shame, and Deep Shame always won.

On this better day there was a rain shower, and after the rain shower the sun broke through the clouds. Calle Sue remembered a day like this at Hannamann Farms. After that long ago day of summer rain when the sun came out and the air was clean and crisp, and she couldn't stay inside a minute longer, she went outside and jump-roped all the way down the wet driveway to the lane gate and back, counting the jumps along the way. Then she remembered another day after the rain when she took Little Otto to the gardens. On that day they picked daisies for Mother, the drops of rain still on the daisies when they brought them to her. Mother hugged them both. With a loving smile on her face she said, "What dear children I have."

Still feeling the warmth of that hug, and remembering the love in Mother's smile, Callie Sue thought her heart would burst. Tears surfaced and spilled over.

Finally allowing herself to fully remember Hannamann Farms, her beautiful secure home, and feeling the deep love she still held for Mother and her dad, and for Anna and Little Otto and Grandmother Lily, the lonesome yearnings pulled together as one. Their strength was immense. More than anything else in the world, Callie Sue wanted to go home.

Do you remember that dismal day when Callie Sue stood at Ozella's window and told herself she had nowhere else to go? ("Other girls go home. Other girls aren't prostitutes.") Now, on this day when *beautiful* stepped up to trump *dismal*, she told herself, "I'm not a prostitute now. I *can* go home."

Before she'd risk just showing up, though, she'd call. She'd find a phone and rev up her courage and call.

It was a red-letter day. After days of agonizing uncertainty Callie Sue made her decision and a heavy weight lifted from her shoulders. In new happiness her thoughts flew ahead to seeing her family soon.

But then…a crash.

Relief and joy ebbed after the call. Callie Sue's confidence waned and she fell into despair. "How can I tell my family the ugly truth?" she asked herself. "What am I thinking? I can't tell them the truth, and I can't possibly go home."

Mulling it over, perceiving her sordid past as a serious threat to the happy homecoming she yearned for and didn't want to give up, she decided to lie. When she called home again she had a story made up about a successful life and career in California. She embellished it with pleasant narratives describing a pretty apartment, respectable friends, even interesting travel. "My family will tell the neighbors and their friends how proud they are," she told herself. "They'll say, 'You know, Callie Sue went through teenage trauma and ran away, but in the end she made something of herself.'"

Even with the support of her lies, though, Callie Sue couldn't bring herself to go home. She couldn't take the next step. Every time she considered going home she put it off. When her mother, on the phone, pushed for when she was coming, she made excuses.

Again, we the unknowing, the unschooled in the dark side of life, the advice-givers, have something to say. Callie Sue should get over it. (Why *doesn't* she get over it?) She should jump at the chance to come home to be darling Callie Sue again, the bubbling energetic girl we remember. She should put on her best smile and say to herself, "Well, I'm off to home now," and get herself to the airport as fast as she can.

Back at Hannamann Farms the family was on a high. In their over-the-top joy of knowing Callie Sue was alive and doing well, in their desperate desire to hold her in their arms, they made an impulsive decision. "If our girl isn't coming home we'll go to her." So with good intentions saturated with naïve innocence, on the next call Eva announced (didn't ask), "We're coming, Callie Sue. We'll see you soon."

Losing no time the entire family, even Grandmother Lily (and Dierdre, too) boarded a plane and flew west to California.

Callie Sue panicked. Pushed to the limit of her confidence and pressed for time she came up with a plan to support her lies. First she'd arrange for the family to stay at a nice hotel, knowing her dad would pay the bill. Then she'd meet them with open arms at the airport, a beautiful happy young woman in tasteful attire, radiating success.

She thought her plan would work, but as she watched her family in the terminal anxiously scanning the waiting crowd she wasn't so sure. Seeing them after so many years was a shock she didn't plan for. There's Mother with her dad, both older now, both smiling and eager. And there's dear Anna, tall now, and precious Little Otto all grown up and handsome, and there's Grandmother Lily, and Dierdre's come as well. Everyone looking expectant and happy.

She doesn't miss the proud. The message is, "We're a proud family and now we'll have our long-lost Callie Sue back and we'll be a proud family together."

"Not really," she thought, shrinking back into the waiting crowd. "I'm their long-lost daughter but if they find out the truth they won't be proud. Imagine them saying, 'Here she is, folks. Step right up. Come and meet Callie Sue, our daughter who's been prostituting in California.'"

Watching her family, Callie Sue could only think, "How innocent they are. They have no idea." And then, "I can't see this working."

But after six years of practicing survival skills and not wanting to give up going home, Callie Sue knew what she had to do. Pulling herself together, she stood up tall and stayed the course. When her family found her she was composed.

To the relief and delight of all, the reunion

began with heartfelt hugs and happy tears.

The second day, though, was another story.

Overwhelmingly distraught and tired, and uneasy living with the lie she'd made up, Callie Sue broke down. She talked, and once she started talking she withheld nothing. It all came out. She told about the abduction, the rapes, the trip across the country to be sold, the terrible beatings, the early years of prostitution on the streets, the later high-end escort life, Ozella's arrest and her arrest.

Tears came as the story broke and then she sobbed, out of control. Occasionally she paused in her confession to gasp at what she was doing but then she was at it again, willing herself to charge ahead and account for every bad memory she could bring back.

For Callie Sue the confession was relief, but for the people she loved it was profound shock. It was like a bucket of ice water thrown on them in one big swoosh. They reeled, deeply stunned.

At first it was too much to believe. "Could this terrible thing happen to our precious Callie Sue? In our quiet community?" Surely not. "On Hannamann property? In Grandmother Lily's house?" Not possible.

But when reality finally showed up, they did believe.

In this case reality was a heavy boulder that rolled in as Callie Sue told her story, crushing the simple and unfounded assumption she was still an innocent child. It lumbered along slowly, ruthlessly spewing out the truth, leaving tear-streaked faces in its path. Also hollow stomachs and abysmal sorrow, to say nothing of complete surprise at the criminal acts. For the Hannamanns, homespun folks who think crime is what you read about in newspapers or watch in movies, this is a shameful thing. This is what happens to other families.

Callie Sue's story was a bitter pill to swallow.

As the real truth emerged the family went into shock. Numb, they drew together seeking solace in each other as they talked and discussed. They struggled first through anger and shame, then through overwhelming sadness. They went down roads they didn't know existed and dug up feelings they didn't know were buried. Finally, with guarded caution they considered, "What do we do now? Where do we go from here?"

This is where I offer a personal opinion. I'm proud of the Hannamanns for their answer to,

"What do we do now?" and "Where do we go from here?" In my mind they did the right thing. Some in our town, if they knew the story, wouldn't allow them credit, instead shrugging their shoulders and pointing out in a dismissive way, "Well, they had no choice."

I, Emma Betz, say they did have a choice. I know the Hannamann ways and I know the Hannamann code of conduct doesn't crack. But this time, thank God, it did crack. The first shock weakened its hard crust of proper decorum and finally the code shattered. There, exposed, was all of the love and kindness and decency and loyalty the family was known for.

As the days of disbelief and struggle melded into days of belief and acceptance, albeit sad belief and acceptance, the family pulled itself together into a binding confirmation of loyalty to Callie Sue.

I'll go on now.

With the direction of action now defined there was planning to do. The family got right to it.

"What about Earle?" came up right away, and right then and there vain Earle Meier, my own pompous shirttail relative, lost the favor he'd enjoyed for years. Until they could deal in earnest with new awareness of his incompetence the family pushed Earle Meier, Elected Sheriff of Hermann County, onto a back burner. It was a unanimous decision. Wise Grandfather Betz, who never did think much of Earle, would have added his vote. He would have said, "Good. The guy's finally getting his comeuppance."

A harder decision waited, this one needing serious discussion. Looming as a huge dilemma was how to deal with the community's inevitable gossip. Given her experience with gossips, Grandmother Lily in particular pushed the issue. She knew the wild glee the gossips would have when they found out that Callie Sue Hannamann, once the notorious darling of the community, spent six years prostituting in California. To say nothing of the rapes. Oh, my. Rapes are only talked about in secret. Rapes are *shameful.*

The community wouldn't be kind. Probably it would condemn. Callie Sue could easily become the community pariah and her sins would be unpardonable.

So when Dierdre finally let go of the *Buck Whoever You Are* story and tearfully shared it, the family decided to put it to good use. They constructed a big lie for the folks back home. *Callie Sue ran away with a man from the road construction at Hanover. Left him after a few years and now has a job in California. No children. Doing well. Seems to be happy.*

When Earle heard the lie he helped it along. He puffed himself up and strutted around and told anyone who would listen that Callie Sue ran away. "Just like I said all along," he crowed.

I give the Hannamanns, especially Grandmother Lily, a gold star for thinking ahead to when Callie Sue would return. Well-schooled in the unwritten but clearly understood rules of our community, Grandmother Lily knew we'd allow running away, albeit with thin lips, on our list of allowable moral infractions. Never, never, would we allow prostitution, even forced prostitution. Don't even ask.

All at the reunion swore themselves to the *Buck Whoever You Are* story. Even Anna and Lo insisted they could keep Callie Sue's secret.

Here's the real story, that isn't a lie.

Already at the bottom of a deep pit with steep sides, after Callie Sue told her story she didn't even try to climb out. She scrunched down in a corner of the pit by herself, in a world no one else could come close to understanding. For six years she'd been abused and violated. Exhausted from trying to stay alive and keeping her family alive, and still confused about why her family didn't look for her, the girl was a mess. Botched up. No matter what was told to the folks back home, Callie Sue wasn't doing well and 'seems to be happy' was about as far away from the truth as a person can get.

In dangerous water, the floating bobber careened wildly up and down and every which way. Recklessly out of control, it threatened to head out to open sea.

Eva and Walter watched their daughter crumbling. They watched her vacillate from quiet tears one day to wild out-of-control sobbing the next day. They saw her cling to Eva like a baby clings to its mother, and they listened with horror to the screams of her nightmares.

Afraid isn't a strong enough word to describe the fear going through their heads.

In desperate straits, frightened, away from home and out of their comfort zone, Eva and Walter made a radical move completely out of character. Setting their feet solid, with serious purpose they searched out therapy for Callie Sue, right there in California. When the family flew back Eva stayed behind with Callie Sue, and when Eva came home later, alone, she and Walter sent monthly checks back to California.

As Callie Sue's therapy stretched into months, back home Eva and Walter struggled with pain. They decided to make quiet trips to California to spend time alone with her, and it was during these times together when they came to fully understand what Callie Sue had been through, grasping the deep emotional cost of her abuse.

It was also during these times alone with Callie Sue when they came to terms with their part in the tragedy. The new understanding brought immense grief and profound heartache. Shedding many tears, Eva and Walter loved Callie Sue more than they ever believed possible, and vowed to never lose her again.

But they did lose her. Not totally, but to some extent. And in an unexpected way.

The day finally arrived when the floating bobber stayed upright and it looked like calm water ahead. It was then, when Callie Sue felt better and could see a future, that she gave Eva and Walter a surprise they didn't like. She told them she wouldn't be coming home to live. She told them she planned to stay in California. She wanted to start a new life. What she didn't tell them: "I need to break away from the tight reins of Hannamann expectations, and I can't live with the stifling community constraints I remember so well."

Eva cried when she heard the news and Walter pleaded with Callie Sue to reconsider, even offered her a partnership in Hannamann Farms if she'd come home. But Callie Sue wouldn't be persuaded.

Since her announcement Callie Sue has stubbornly held her ground. Indeed, she's taken up residence in California, although she comes home occasionally for visits. To Eva and Walter's dismay, she chooses to make the visits short.

Four Years After Bondage

2007

"We shall draw from the heart of suffering itself
the means of inspiration and survival."

– Winston Churchill

I'm skipping ahead now, in Callie Sue's story. It's been four years since Ozella's arrest. I can't begin to cover the ups and downs Callie Sue's lived through in the four years, or deal with the trials and unease of her family. Even if I tried to report Callie Sue's ups and downs or talk about the pain her family endured, the narratives would add little to the story.

What I can say is this. The Hannamanns are learning to live with what happened. Each family member is making a personal journey toward acceptance. Some have found peace but others continue to struggle.

If we look in from the outside it appears the family's faring well. But this is a misleading observation because we know Hannamanns always keep up appearances, and at all costs. From past behavior we can speculate that appearances out at Hannamann Farms don't tell the real story.

I know the real story, and I'll share it with you here.

As she was determined to do, Callie Sue stayed in California. She's working on the new life she wants. You'll be interested to know that at twenty-four she's still stunningly beautiful and yes, she still "likes pretty things," as Eva once said, so it shouldn't surprise us that her interest is in the field of fashion. Right now Callie Sue's putting her heart and soul into finishing her education because she wants to design and market trendy clothes, a goal that fits well with her creative talents. Eva and Walter support Callie Sue in every way, including paying for her schooling and living expenses.

There's a change in Callie Sue's approach to life. She isn't the bubbly exuberant girl we once knew, filled with the energy and zest of her growing up years. Hard to believe but she's quiet now, and watchful. One wouldn't go so far as to call her a recluse but when she comes for visits she stays out at the farm, only venturing away to drive into Hamburg to the library or visit Grandmother Lily at Quiet Haven. She isn't interested in renewing friendships in the community, or in seeking out new challenges here.

The Hannamann Farms routines have eased back in. But here is a change as well. A different atmosphere prevails out at the farm now, unnoticed if you didn't know the Hannamanns earlier when the atmosphere was decidedly confident and happy. Now the joy of having Callie Sue back is tempered with a kind of unspoken sadness. Not dismal gloomy sadness with downcast eyes and cheerless days but melancholy sadness, quietly and persistently finding its way into everyday living.

There are scars. (How could there not be scars?) Some are deep and still fester. Some are faded and some are purposely buried, but for sure they're there.

Eva and Walter's scars are deep and there's no doubt they still fester. Still hard on themselves, they rue should haves and shouldn't haves. "We should have celebrated Callie Sue's talents. We shouldn't have trusted Earle Meier. We shouldn't have rented Grandmother Lily's house to smooth-talking strangers." The list goes on, and every day the festering scars cause pain. Behind the façade of 'everything's fine', Eva and Walter Hannamann carry heavy burdens.

You ask about the children. And you wonder about Grandmother Lily. "What about their scars?" you ask.

I can tell you about the children. And I can tell you about Grandmother Lily.

True to who she is, Anna's scars are buried. Purposely buried. The relationship between Anna and Callie Sue is harmonious but the two sisters aren't close. This isn't surprising given Callie Sue's long absence and the innate differences in temperament. And remember too, that Anna lived a long time in the shadow of 'Waiting for Callie Sue', an uncomfortable place she didn't accept, ever. After coming to terms with her goals Anna finished her junior high school and high school years with exemplary grades and left Hannamann Farms for college. With Connor still in the picture she's making a life for herself. Always sensible and independent, Anna does what it takes to find her own way. "I'm doing fine, thank you," meaning, "I'm doing fine by myself, thank you," is still Anna Hannamann's modus operandi.

I'm happy to report that Lo is still the sweet dear boy he always was. His scars have faded, along with the fantasy of living with Callie Sue. She isn't his constant companion now but the two are inseparable when she visits. If anyone in the family gets a medal for loyalty it's Lo, and Callie Sue still watches over her little brother with ownership. When she's home she clues him in about the dangers of the world, sitting him down and lecturing in his face. About the locket, she can't bear to look at it. Seeing it brings back unwanted memories of the terrible time in Grandmother Lily's house, calling up the day she hid the locket in the dresser cubbyhole. It was her last desperate hope for a rescue. Callie Sue can't bear to look at the locket and Lo can't bear to part with the locket. So he still keeps it in his treasure box, away from her eyes. They both know it's there...a never-spoken-about reminder of a deeply painful time.

As Callie Sue struggled with therapy in California, back home Grandmother Lily struggled with a stroke. Here in the community our hearts go out to her. Lily Hannamann's been with us a long time and we've come to love her kind ways as well as smile at her acerbic tongue. She lost Otto, then Callie Sue, and if that wasn't enough sadness, our good friend was hit with a major stroke. Callie Sue wonders if the stroke is somehow connected to what happened to her. To be honest, a lot of people wonder about it, only they don't just wonder. They're *pretty sure* the stroke is linked to 'that spoiled girl who ran away', which is not a fair reading at all but there you are. Stories get started. Anyhow, on her visits to Hannamann Farms Callie Sue pushes her grandmother's wheelchair out to the grounds of Quiet Haven. There's a garden gazebo there now, built as a memorial to Otto. After he died the family cast about for how to use the large sum of memorial money. Seems that Otto collected friends like he collected land and his friends wanted to honor him. Since Otto planned to live at Quiet Haven with Lily in their old age, building a gazebo on the grounds was what she wanted to do with the money. Callie Sue and Grandmother Lily sit in the gazebo reminiscing, recalling Callie Sue's growing up days and the happy times they had together. We see them there, an old woman clutching beloved memories to her heart and a young woman delighting in a stronghold of her childhood that's still strong...that of her grandmother's unconditional love.

And then there's Dierdre.

Dierdre's dropped back. If she's scarred, by golly she won't admit it. She and Callie Sue talk but they aren't tight. Instead, they walk a narrow path of friendship that seems to work for both. What can I say? Callie Sue's moved on to another world and Dierdre's staying in her own world. Still farming, still breaking rules, still roaring around in her convertible. Wouldn't you know, she bought herself a creamy white hardtop, undeniably classy, which gives the wags new material. "Dierdre got herself another convertible," they faithfully report, "and that wild woman has a heavy foot on the gas pedal of this one, too." Both aware of never-ending gossip but ignoring it, Eva and Dierdre continue their coffee parties every week at Dierdre's kitchen table. As before, Walter doesn't approve. The family's still put out with Dierdre for sitting on the *Buck Whoever You Are* story when she should have been forthcoming, and they don't forgive her. Especially Walter and Grandmother Lily are unforgiving. But Eva doesn't dwell on it. She stubbornly and willfully keeps her friendship with Dierdre going because the tie that binds, for many years weak, is now strong. Eva aims to keep it that way.

Scars show up in Hannamann lives and they also have a hand in dictating Hannamann gatherings. Or lack thereof. Gatherings of the clan stopped when Callie Sue disappeared and they didn't get started again. Every year Callie Sue was in bondage Eva said, "I can't do this. I don't want to do this," and she still says, "I can't do this. I don't want to do this." She gives herself all manner of excuses. "Anyhow Grandfather Otto isn't here to hold court with his prayers and that would be sad and the Callie Sue thing might cast a shadow and the real story might slip out and what a catastrophe that would be. And I wouldn't want to invite Earle and hear him spout off like a gushing geyser and people would wonder why he wasn't invited and I wouldn't care to explain." She adds a final *and* that gives little hope the gatherings will be reinstated. With tears in her eyes, Eva says with suspicious finality, "and maybe I'll never again want to do this."

The community watches. Even as time passes and memories fade, it watches and keeps track.

It watches like an eagle hovering overhead, ever looking for something juicy to feast on. People say, "Nice to see you, Callie Sue," Or, "You say you're in California now?" They're hinting in a roundabout way for information, their casual questions making it look like they care. But I know better. They might care but it's clear to me they're also hankering for more dirt.

As for the real gossips, they try to keep the embers of a once-glowing fire alive, but they have little fuel for that fire. The family and I, Emma Betz, continue to be closemouthed.

Realizing right away on her first visit back to Hannamann Farms she no longer fits with her friends, Callie Sue doesn't want to spend time with them. In her aloneness she drives into Hamburg to the library to check out a book or two. When I saw Callie Sue in the library that first time I knew right away the girl was alone in the world. It was written all over her…from her subdued face to the way she kept her head down and cleverly hid herself between the shelves, not wanting to talk to anyone.

She seemed surprised when I made an effort to reach out, but grateful and appreciative. We've struck up a friendship. "An unlikely friendship," you say, but remember I'm reliable and people trust me. Callie Sue trusts me, and on my side I've grown fond of

Callie Sue. When she comes back to Hannamann Farms we meet for coffee after the library closes for the day. Or we drive the fifteen miles to Hanover for dinner. There's a quiet restaurant there we like, out at the edge of town. We sit in a back booth, just the two of us.

Callie Sue talks and I listen. She tells me what she can't tell her parents. She tells me the details of her abduction, and about the squalid world of sex and brutal violence where she struggled to stay alive. She tells me about her feelings when she was trying to stay alive. How she trusted no one and had no real friends. About how bad she felt, and about how sometimes she curled up in a little ball in a corner by herself, crying and hugging her knees. She tells me how ashamed she was, and the shame's still there and she hates it. She tells me that sometimes she hates herself.

Often Callie Sue's in tears but more often we cry together. And after our times together I come home thinking about the conversations, marveling at this girl's courage.

"I think my family will always struggle with what happened," Callie Sue says with tears in her eyes, "and I think Mother and my dad will stay on the same rutted paths." I agree, but with reservation. Like Callie Sue, I think her family will always struggle.

But unlike Callie Sue, I know how time heals. So I'll give some hope for healing to more passage of time.

Callie Sue's right about her parents staying on the same rutted paths. Why wouldn't they? Hannamanns don't like change. But there *is* a change in the paths. They continue on but the ruts aren't as deep, and if we look carefully we'll see some of them angling off course.

I tell Callie Sue this, and I also tell her not to fret because some of the paths are wonderfully constant. I tell her that to people looking in her dad's still the best farmer in the community and her mother still works in the community for every good cause. Grandmother Lily still turns her back to the gossips, Anna goes her own way, and Lo is as sweet as always.

But I also point out that people looking in see Hannamanns who've become less judgmental. They see Hannamanns who make an effort to understand those who break out of the mold. "Callie Sue, this is a good thing," I say.

When I say, "This is a good thing," Callie Sue smiles but she doesn't respond.

Finally, I tell Callie Sue her family's doing the best they can. Although some in the family, particularly Eva and Walter, still struggle to accept what happened, right now they're doing a good job of living with what happened. From what I see, the family's giving life its best shot.

Callie Sue's doing the same. It's the way she is. It's the way she was when she was growing up on Hannamann Farms and it's the way she was in bondage, and it's the way she is now. She didn't throw in the towel during the desperate times and she isn't throwing in the towel now.

Callie Sue's trying hard. We can depend on it. You bet your boots we can depend on it.

As wise Grandfather Betz would have said, "By golly, Emma, we can take it to the bank."

Emma Betz here…again.

So now I've said what I had to say. I've said it plain and simple the way it came down, without getting things out of kilter.

I don't mind admitting that writing Callie Sue's story was a more intense labor than I planned for. For one thing, there was emotional involvement I didn't expect. The emotional involvement took a lot out of me when I was writing, and it still does.

The thing is, I've come to be close to the Hannamanns. I've been getting close to their lives, getting inside their heads, trying to be honest about what they went through, and I've gotten myself connected. Sometime during my writing these well-meaning people became like my own family. Who wouldn't be proud to have the Hannamanns for family? They're the finest people I know. I've come to think highly of these hardworking folks who for years tried to do the right thing, minded their own business, and then got hit with heartbreaking tragedy.

The Hannamanns don't know they have an ardent supporter right here in town. I've kept my distance and I aim to keep doing just that, but keeping my distance doesn't mean I don't care. I care very much.

And what about Callie Sue? What *about* this young woman, this innocent victim of sinister evil? What's in store for her?

I'd like to say she has clear sailing ahead but we don't know this to be true. We do know things can go up or down in the aftermath of an ugly experience, and Callie Sue's experience was about as ugly as it gets.

I'm the first to say Callie Sue's come a long way in the right direction but I'm also the first to say she's still healing. I say give her more time, and add in a generous amount of forbearance and patience. Some prayers would be in order as well.

As for me, Emma Betz, I can't let Callie Sue go. When all is said and done, she's far too close to my heart to walk away. I've decided that for as long as Callie Sue comes back to Hannamann Farms and comes into the library, and for as long as we're still friends, I'll be here for her.

I'll know how she's doing because I'll keep track. I'll make it my business to keep track. When Callie Sue comes in I'll see if she stands tall or slumps her shoulders. I'll see if she steps right out or hangs back and drags her feet, and for sure I'll see if she stays out in the open or heads for the back shelves where she can hide.

And I'll watch her when an old friend comes near. Right now, someone she knew years ago will walk toward her, maybe just wanting to say hello in a friendly way, and Callie Sue purposely buries herself in a book or looks out the window to avoid eye contact. I've seen her purposely turn her back to a person and walk to my desk to talk.

So yes, you can be sure I'll keep track.

And you can be sure that all the while I'm keeping track I'll be pulling with everything I have for this fine, brave, precious young woman who's crawled into my heart and become my friend.

And you can take that to the bank, too.

THE END

CPSIA information can be obtained
at www.ICGtesting.com
Printed in the USA
FSHW021626130421
80416FS